BY WAY OF PAIN

Criminal Delights: Assassins

J.M. DABNEY

Copyright © 2019 by J.M. Dabney

Hostile Whispers Press, LLC

ISBN-13: **978-1-947184-27-5**

Edits by AlternativEdits (Laura McNellis & Stephanie Carrano)

Cover by: Natasha Snow

REMEMBER:

This book is a work of fiction. All characters, places, and events are from the author's imagination and should not be confused with fact. Any resemblance to persons, living or dead, events or places, is purely coincidental.

PLEASE BE ADVISED:

This book contains material that is only suitable for mature readers. It may contain scenes of a sexual nature and violence.

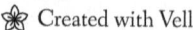 Created with Vellum

DOUBLE LIVES WERE JUST THE WAY IT WAS FOR A MAN LIKE ME.

By day I was a man with a reputation above reproach. Even assassins needed backup plans. For fifteen years, life was going without a hitch until I had to take out a witness. When it was time to kill him, beautiful eyes filled with fear urged me to do something else. Yet, in order to do that, I had to break him, and by way of pain, my captive would experience pleasure he'd never dreamed.

This book is part of CRIMINAL DELIGHTS. Each novel can be read as a standalone and contains a dark M/M romance.

Warning: These books are for adult readers who enjoy stories where lines between right and wrong get blurry. High heat, twisted and tantalizing, these are not for the fainthearted.

Trigger Warnings: Title contains the following possible triggers. Humiliation, Violence, Master/slave elements, Male Chastity, Murder, Imprisonment, Dub-Con, and Torture.

It is always by way of pain one arrives at pleasure.
—Marquis De Sade (1740 - 1840)

To the readers because without every one of you I wouldn't be here to tell my stories. You are all amazing.

Special thanks to all the people who made this book possible, who kept me going when all I wanted to do was quit. Tracey, Stephanie, Meredith, Jenn, Laura, and all the betas who helped me to make this the best book possible. All of you help me to be better.

PROLOGUE

Patient: Cowen Kingsley – Age 8

My weekly appointment with Dr. Parelli commenced five minutes ago and started the same way. My blank stare was boring into him. My parents were frightened of me. I saw it every day. If it had been up to me, I wouldn't have survived to take my first breath. With my fingers laced together, I sneakily stroked my thumb over the bandage on my wrist. They'd caught me before I had a chance to succeed at killing myself.

"How are you feeling today, Cowen?" The doctor put on his best friendly smile. All false caring as he prepared to test me. I knew that's what he did. The conversations were there in black and white, transcribed pages in his doctor's scrawl. I'd broken in and listened to each one of the tapes. They never failed to end with a tentative recommendation of commitment to a long-term facility.

I carefully studied him as I analyzed the inquiry about my feelings and I didn't know how to answer. I sat up straighter in my seat. He'd tried to get me to lie down on the couch—to relax and trust him that he'd make me all better.

As far as I was concerned, nothing was wrong with me. I didn't care what anyone said. This was me for as long as I could remember.

"How did you get along with your classmates this week?"

When he realized that I wasn't going to answer him, he moved on to another line of questioning. They'd discussed it and decided to send me to public school. A behavioral exercise to attempt to teach me to relate to my peers—learn empathy. I found my fellow students abhorrent. The way they processed things with their feeble minds confused me.

"Acceptable."

"Cowen, your parents told me about an incident. Why don't you tell me your side of it?"

The principal had singled me out. As much as I loathed the other kids, they were only a product of their parents. The adults should know better. The incident that the doctor spoke of had quickly been swept away by a quickly-written check.

"I didn't like him."

"It had to be more than that. We have to find out your triggers in order to figure out how to process them in a healthy manner."

"He intruded on my personal space. I warned him before I stabbed him with a letter opener."

"We've spoken about this. Hurting others isn't the proper response. You state the need for your personal space and people will respect it. Positive reinforcement—"

I zoned out. Why change when my method worked just as well and left a lasting impression. My parents had made it possible to continue with my life without a permanent record or at least one that seemed normal to the outside world. Except I knew they were just waiting for the right moment to lock me up and forget about me.

For now, my actions were manageable, nothing they couldn't pay people to forget.

"Cowen, tell me about your suicide attempt. This is your second one in two years or were you just trying to self-harm?"

"No, I tried to kill myself, but they found me too soon. Next time I'll make sure I'm alone."

Alone time was rare because someone was always watching me. I could pretend to be normal long enough for them to let down their guard. They were stupid enough to be manipulated. It wouldn't be too hard.

He set his legal pad aside and leaned forward, resting his elbows on his knees, and I didn't like how close he was to me.

"Cowen, all I want to do is help. Whatever is said in this room will stay between us. We need to develop trust between us so that I can help you. Do you want to live the rest of your life like this?"

I didn't answer, but it was there on the tip of my tongue. Yes, I wanted to be just like this.

~~~~~

PATIENT: COWEN KINGSLEY – AGE 16

His screams were muffled by the balled-up socks I'd stuffed in his mouth as I stood in front of him. I calmly stood and read the newest report. Unlike the ones before, this one included commitment papers, signed by Dr. Parelli and my parents.

"Recommended for immediate commitment as of

October twelfth, signed and witnessed by you and my parents. Now, now, doctor, I thought everything that was said in this office stayed between us."

I waited as if I expected him to answer and the yells rose in volume as I gifted him another slash to his face. I used the bloody tip of my knife to move down the sheet. "Suicidal tendencies. Compulsive self-harm. Psychopathic personality. Narcissistic. Wow, I'm surprised you didn't run out of paper outlining my many disorders."

I'd broken into his office just after he'd turned the sign. Picking the lock was easy enough. My parents were currently knocked out from the sedatives I'd slipped into their evening drinks. I noticed the dim light of the desk lamp hitting off the many marks on my forearm, the new ones still seeped blood, and the remembered pain grounded me for the moment.

"Anything to say for yourself, *doctor*? You had plenty to say about *me*, so let's continue shall we." I eased down in the chair I'd placed beside him. "It is my belief that he will be a danger to society and will never live a productive life. If I had feelings, I'd almost be hurt." I placed the blade under his chin and tipped his head back.

"It's people like you who make the unique among us insecure about what is natural for us. Have you seen the hellscape that is our world, doctor? Who are you to say that my homicidal tendencies aren't a service to the population?"

I loathed society and everything about it. I'd tried to leave it all behind, and all that happened was I'd woken up in the hospital sewn back together. People assumed it was a way to garner attention, but I cared nothing about the opinions of others. The discomfort people felt around me had resulted in me being taken out of school and taught at home.

They all waited for the day I killed, wouldn't they love to know that the doctor wouldn't be my first. I'd slit the throat of a man on the street years before. After I'd done it, I'd crouched down beside him in the alley and watched the life slowly drain from his eyes. Tears had flowed down his temples into his dark, unkempt hair. It had been exhilarating, and nothing had made me feel the same since.

"Oh, let us not forget this little tidbit. Sexual sadist. How did we come to believe that I would endure a vulgar act such as sex?"

I felt no pull toward men or women. When I was in school, everyone talked about sex, and I had no compulsion or interest in lowering myself to my baser instincts. Pain was all I needed.

"Do you know that my parents are next? Oh, not right now, but once I'm eighteen, I've planned it down to the minute detail. And with all the files and tapes of our sessions disappearing there won't be one single piece of evidence. I'll be the perfect angel for the next two years."

I drew the blade across his throat and watched the skin split in a macabre display as his blood turned his pristine white shirt crimson. Sitting there, I watched until he bled to death bound and gagged on the floor. After he slumped and the last of his life was gone, I removed the evidence that I ever existed. If there was one thing I knew in life, it was how to remove my existence. I was nothing, a mistake of nature and I could accept that when no one else could.

Chapter One

COWEN

T he rich scent of cologne filled my nostrils as my personal assistant traversed my office organizing the day's paperwork. His broad body was big and slightly soft around the middle. I'd hired Harrison three years before when his predecessor retired. I'd hesitated to offer the man the position because the moment I saw him, I imagined him chained as my whip met the width of his back. Wanting to hurt a man made me rethink allowing them close. I never entertained the notion of fucking people.

I lived a double life. By day, I ran a very successful one-person law firm that specialized in criminal law. The irony of being a defense attorney wasn't lost on me. At night, I killed whomever my employer required or when I was bored and took a freelance assignment. I only killed those I felt unworthy of the life they were given. Civilians were strictly off-limits, but that didn't mean I wouldn't if the opportunity called for it. Killing was something I'd accepted since I was six and imagined slitting my teacher's throat. I'd never questioned the thoughts that filled my head. My parents were so frightened of me that I'd visited more psychiatrists than I could count by the time I started kindergarten. They tested me for everything, IQ to psychoses, yet hadn't subjected me to therapy until I was seven.

Guilt was an emotion I'd never experienced. I'd always considered emotion a waste of energy. I'd accepted the depraved thing I was long ago, and I had no qualms about remaining that way.

The only joy I received from my existence was killing. I took pride in my work and inflicting pain was my skill. My employer didn't care how I dispatched them as long as he had proof that I'd completed my job. He didn't give a fuck about my bit of fun. I didn't follow the societal rules of decorum. If I wanted to take a life, I didn't think twice about the consequences. Nearly forty years and hundreds of bodies later, I'd settled into the life that worked best for a monster such as myself.

I'd lived a celibate life for years now. Sex just didn't give me any pleasure. When I found a mark who was aesthetically pleasing, their pain was enough in a sense to get me off. I didn't have orgasms, the contentment I received from inflicting torture was fleeting but enough. My assistant made me rethink my sexless existence, but not enough to chain him in my bedroom to use as I saw fit.

Evading capture for as long as I had was due to the fact that I had steadfast rules. And forming attachments broke my number one tenet I followed. My two lives were compartmentalized in such a way neither would ever intrude on the other. A toy would open me to speculation I didn't welcome.

I placed my elbows on the arms of my desk chair and steepled my fingers, pressing the sides to my lips. Although, as much as I denied my darkest desires, it didn't mean that I hadn't imagined the beast of a man on his knees for me. His broad back stretched his ill-fitted suit jacket. It was cheap and off the rack. His pants were much too loose. The giant of a man screamed submissive from the sweetness of his soft-spoken nature to his habit of averting his gaze. It would be almost too easy to break him. My pretty assistant didn't pose the challenge I craved. His spirit would shatter much too quickly to make the experience fun for me.

People would call me a psychopath and a sadist. After I'd killed my psychiatrist when I was sixteen when he attempted to have me committed, I'd perused my records with great interest. He'd labeled me a danger to society. His recommendation stated I should never be allowed out of a maximum-security facility.

The soft ping of my second phone drew my attention, and I picked it up. I read the coded message. I mentally decoded the single sentence and made note of where and when. I'd arrive at a drop point later tonight and pick up a package with target information including a photo.

I felt the uneasy feeling of a gaze on me and jerked my head up. Harrison looked away and pretended to work. The last task he needed to complete should already be done.

"Have you finished for the day?"

My question had his shoulders tightening. He seemed to steel himself for a blow, and as it had happened over the years, his timidity elicited a curiosity to which I rarely succumbed. My inappropriate imaginings about him caused me to want to hurt whoever caused him to drawback or brace himself. The part of my brain that wanted him and felt that no one else should touch him tortured me.

"Yes, sir."

His deep voice shook a little over the word sir. I demanded a level of dictatorial professionalism. Too many times over the years, I've seen men such as myself taken down by letting their cover make them soft. I had no intentions of giving up my life. I didn't experience emotion like other people. My emotional cues were practiced in the mirror. I responded as was expected, but a smile to me was simply a muscle reaction—I mimicked expressions yet felt nothing of what they conveyed.

"Then why are you still here?"

He couldn't escape the confines of my office any quicker, and once again, the pleasure I took in his fear filled me with a rare warmth. The movements in the outer office helped me track his path until the lock on the door clicked. I was sure I was alone and unfolded my lean body from my chair. Pivoting on my toes, I stared out over the city.

It was a place created for a hunter. Big, sprawling and dirty—victims roaming the streets unaware of their status as prey. They all felt they were safe from the monsters because they were all easily spotted, but they knew nothing about my kind. We were just an abstract concept on some true crime show they watched in the middle of the night—evil reduced to caricature. My reputation was above reproach, but I was the most prolific killer of my kind.

In moments of respite where I hid away in my cabin, I'd analyzed when I'd become broken. I believed my sociopathy was a result of conception. Maybe something as damaged as I shouldn't have survived to birth. A shell without a soul. I'd attempted suicide a time or two, and I bore the marks from years of self-harm. I'd hoped to feel something—pain proved you were alive—and yet the more I cut and burned, it became nothing more than a minor inconvenience—wounds to heal.

I closed my eyes, drew oxygen in through my nose and

pushed it slowly past my lips, repeated until I opened my eyes. As with any normal person ending work, I gathered up files and my laptop, stowing them inside my satchel briefcase. Everything in my life was routine and repetition, nothing deviated. I arrived at my office at six in the morning and promptly left at six at night. Meetings were scheduled as needed. I appeared in court. I was successful at my chosen cover, but as with all aspects of my existence, they were disguises.

The person I truly was deep down—that's who I hid from all I came across. I turned off all the lights as I made my way out of my office. It was time to make my way to the pickup point. When I exited the building, I categorized my surroundings. I knew every inch of this part of town by heart. Strangers weren't a common sight.

No unfamiliar cars or people loitering about, a group of teenagers who took up post in front of the bodega across the street pretended to be more dangerous than they were. Arrogance was a downfall. The quickest way to underestimating your opponent was to think you were superior in battle.

At a safe distance, I pushed the remote start on my key fob and waited a few minutes before I approached to open the door. I tossed my briefcase to the passenger side and slid onto the driver's seat. Even as it appeared that I wasn't, I paid attention to the view outside the windows of my vehicle. The place I'd find my assignment packet was a secluded spot in the city's central park.

This time of day before dinner, the park was filled with people doing their evening runs. Stenton was on the cusp of fall, still holding onto the warmth of late summer and everyone took advantage before the brutal winters started. I signaled to take the turn into the parking area and got out. I removed my tie and jacket, rolled the sleeves of my dress shirt over my scarred forearms.

To everyone else, I was just another businessman taking a stroll after a long day at the office. I inhaled the fresh scent of cut grass and took the path to a bench near a pond in an isolated corner of the area. It was all so cliched really. The clandestine, hidden envelope would be destroyed in my fireplace after I'd committed the details to memory. If I had a sense of humor, I might even find all of this comical, but that was also another sign of humanity I didn't quite get.

I sat down, crossed my legs to rest my left ankle on my right knee and curled my hand under the edge of the seat. The package gave with only the slightest of pressure. I didn't think to open it. I enjoyed the silence of the moment hidden away in a copse of trees where no one had yet started to clear the leaves from the cobblestone paths. The shimmering gradient of the dying sunset playing across the crisp water fascinated me for a few moments, yet boredom quickly grew.

I stood and headed back to my vehicle, deciding on stopping to pick up dinner on the way home.

Cooking wasn't one of the menial tasks that I enjoyed. Yes, I knew how to cook, but only because I tried to camouflage myself. Tried to learn tasks other normal people found enjoyable. It served me well. But how much longer could I stave off the inevitable need for more? Killing was routine, it meant no more to me than the fleeting pleasure I received from it, but I'd lost count of the bodies. Faceless specters forgotten just as quickly as the life drained from their eyes.

I'd made Stenton my base of operation, but I traveled everywhere to complete my jobs. Nothing kept me in one place, how long would the killing sustain me before I no longer had that? I'd exterminated the last of my biological ties to this world decades ago. Everyone who crossed my path, the ones who might remember me were taken out with no more remorse than the strangers I assassinated. I took pride in my work. My hands were stained with blood and everything in me blackened and rotten. I was born a monster with my fate sealed the second I cried out with my first breath.

Chapter Two

HARRISON

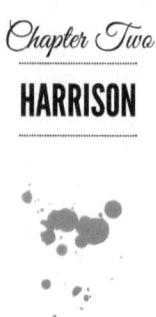

I stroked the angel carved into sun-warmed stone. I placed the cheap grocery store bouquet atop it. Pain and loneliness took me to my knees.

"Hi, Mom."

I cleaned the debris from around her headstone. Granted there wasn't much, I'd been here a week before, and the week before that. Friday evenings I always visited her to tell her about my week. Even five years later, I still missed her. Until I was twenty-five, she and I were the only people we had. She'd withered away over the years. The cancer had started taking her from me when I was thirteen. Her numerous remissions were only brief months of respite. We tried to act as if life were normal while she was healthy. Yet, we knew it would all end with one blood test. Her genetic predisposition to cancer had turned out to be a death sentence.

We'd lived on borrowed time, and while I was thankful her pain ended, in my selfishness, I'd wanted her to hold on just a bit longer.

"I hate my job," I whispered into the breeze that caressed across my face. The tsking and weak chuckle in my head caused me to smile for the first time in days. "I know. First job, I was lucky to get it with no job experience."

I'd acted as caretaker for her so long. Locked away in the house, losing friends even though the night nurse allowed me some semblance of freedom. I felt guilty on my nights out, laughing and drinking with my dwindling friend group.

Sometimes, I thought the scent of death clung to me and they'd sensed it; infected them with a dark cloud with no silver lining. I didn't blame them. They'd gone on to find partners, get married, some had families. Others moved away, and I witnessed their lives through social media posts.

Routine got me through over the years but being alone turned out to be unbearable. Lonely and touch starved. I hadn't realized how the passing time had changed me. My natural shyness had morphed into an awkwardness that I found hard to get over.

I'd known I was gay from an earlier age, came out to my mother, but dating wasn't easy for me. I knew what people thought when they looked at me. Big and scary, looked like one of those alpha Bears who could take charge with their dominance. My confidence hadn't grown into my appearance. It wasn't that I didn't think of myself as attractive. With the scruffy beard that I tried to keep trimmed, people called me handsome and nice. I wasn't the type of man people called sexy or labeled as a bad boy. That distinction didn't fit, and despite appearances, I considered myself submissive. For me, that's why I assumed Mr. Kingsley affected me the way he did and that embarrassed me when I was around him.

No one wanted the nice guy. As I'd had to step into an

adult role when I was barely in my teens, I'd always felt as if my emotional growth had stopped.

"Mr. Kingsley isn't the nicest man, but I can pay the bills and take care of our house. I even paid off the mortgage last week, and I'm almost done with the medical bills. I was thinking of going to Ireland next year as we'd always talked about doing."

I pulled up the delicate weeds and placed the small pile in a plastic shopping bag.

"I think he's an important man and is just stressed out, but he's always so cold. He barely talks to me." I paused as if I was waiting for her to speak to me and make it all better. "I miss you. The house is so quiet, and then I go to work, it's almost as silent, if not for answering the phone. Maybe I need to find a new job."

It wasn't the first time I'd thought about changing employment. Maybe work in a bigger office where I could find friends or at least find people for small talk. I grew sick of hearing my own voice. To be honest, I felt pathetic. I was about to turn thirty and had nothing but a job I wasn't happy going to and then coming home to an empty house. I knew I had more than others, but again, I was selfish and dreamed of more.

"I was thinking about getting a pet. What do you think? Maybe a senior dog. A cat would probably be better...they wouldn't be bothered by being left alone during the day. I'd hate for them to feel lonely."

It continued like that for an hour before I whispered my goodbyes and told her I loved her. I approached my car—it was a sedan that was quickly falling apart. I'd bought it when I was sixteen with the money my mother had saved up for me from my dad's insurance policy. I loved to cook but wasn't ready to head home yet and preparing a meal for one seemed like too much effort. On my drive toward a diner near my place, I let my mind wander.

My namesake was just a man in pictures and stories my mother loved to share with me. He'd been a cop, and my mom had told me he loved being in uniform and walking a beat. He'd known the names of everyone in the neighborhood. Asked about their spouses and kids. She'd told me so many times over the years that I was exactly like him. He'd been a big guy, kind of soft and she claimed that she'd never seen him without a smile. One day, he'd gone to work like normal and had a heart attack. There hadn't been any sign that something was wrong with his heart.

They'd met in high school. She'd been new in the city and Dad was the popular golden boy who played on every sports team they offered. He'd asked her to a homecoming dance out of the blue, and after that, her stories sounded like fairy tales.

I loved when she'd told them. I wanted someone to love me like that. But the big three-o was speeding toward me, and I had yet to even have a date. People had sworn by those dating apps, and while I'd gotten messages, I wanted more than someone who just wanted a body for a few hours.

It all seemed pointless, and I figured I was young enough I had time. Yet didn't my parents prove that time was relative? No one was guaranteed tomorrow, hell, not even the next minute. It just took a split-second, and it all ended.

The despondency which was taking over caused me to be angry at myself. I pulled into the small parking lot and took the last empty spot. The diner was one of those unique places that had survived because it was a neighborhood staple. It was a decommissioned railroad car with tiny booths and an old-fashioned counter. The kitchen was open, and you could watch your food being made.

I got out of my car and wished I'd taken the time to go home to change. The clothes I wore for work were thrift store or clearance rack specials, ill-fitting and worn. I felt shabby in comparison to my boss whose suits looked to cost more than I earned a month.

I made my way inside and took a seat at the counter, placed my drink and food order, and smiled at the waitress who'd already started writing as soon as I walked in.

Sipping at my iced tea, thoughts of my boss came, and I was helpless to ignore them. He was an attractive man with an elegant stature, lean and perfect. I assumed him to be in his late thirties, maybe early forties but his face bore no wrinkles, and his hair was still dark chestnut waves. He didn't seem to be the type to dye his hair. I always pictured him as self-assured—a man who knew his place, and his implied arrogance, I assumed that to be a lofty place. My attraction to my boss made it so much more discomforting to deal with him daily.

I always worried he'd notice my attention. A glance that lasted a second too long. I didn't know if he was gay or not. In the three years that I'd worked for him, I'd never once seen him have a personal visitor. He didn't ask me to make dinner reservations that didn't correspond to a business meeting. His ring finger didn't bear an indent.

"So, how are you, cutie?"

Freda leaned her fleshy hip against the counter and settled in to talk to me as she always did when I stopped in for a meal. Maybe that's why I enjoyed coming here. The nice woman always made time to have a conversation with me.

"I'm good. Harold treating you right?"

Harold and Freda had run the Stenton Station Diner since it opened in the sixties. Part of the charm of the place was watching the husband and wife duo playfully argue. Other than their children who helped out on occasion, the place was a two-person operation.

"I threaten to divorce the man a hundred times a day, you know that. But that would just be cruel. He couldn't do better."

I laughed with her through snippets of conversation, my meal, and the dessert I splurged on so I could stay a few minutes longer. I was isolated and wouldn't deny it, yet I also didn't want to admit it to anyone. Feigning happiness was something I'd done for so long that I didn't know whether it was real or a figment of my imagination.

When I would walk inside the house, the lock clicking into place would have it all come back in blaring clarity. At least here or at work, I could pretend I wasn't alone. That someone would miss me if I didn't appear one day. Would they worry? Probably not. I'd be just another regular who disappeared—found another place to go for their meals or a new place to collect a paycheck.

Without an excuse to stay longer, I threw money on the counter to cover my meal and a generous tip. By the time I walked outside, the cool night breeze had blown away the smell of greasy spoon and strong coffee.

On occasion, I thought about testing my theory, just pack up and go away for a while. Only fear kept me from doing so. It wasn't about the unknown or what existed outside of the city, but the fear my disappearance would be nothing more than a momentary blip. A split-second thought of where was he now.

I hated being depressed. Hating knowing that I was that dispensable. A forgettable part of the scenery. I shoved my hands in the deep pant pockets, and my steps were slow as I strode back to my car. Home was only a five-minute ride, and I dreaded it so much. I wanted someone who would miss me, mourn me when I'm gone, and yet I knew I'd just be a vague and fading memory.

Chapter Three

COWEN

It was Saturday, a few weeks since I'd received the assignment. Some people thought assassins just went right out to take out our victim, but there was planning involved. I leaned against a lamp post across the street from my target's office building. The neighborhood was the perfect spot. Minimal foot traffic. Semi-upscale section. Plenty of alleys on either side. I didn't bother remembering his name past the point of finding him. I knew some who kept mementos of their kills. A tiny reminder, but that was evidence and a stupid serial killer mistake. They got off on reliving the kills. I only needed the moment the life drained from my mark.

I casually smoked a cigarette. I'd given up the habit a decade ago, but no one really paid attention to some guy in a suit having a smoke on the curb. I'd always smoked to blend. Enjoying it was never part of it; just something other people did and I was curious as to why. I snubbed out the smoke and pocketed the filter so as not to leave DNA. The light was slowly dying as dusk moved seamlessly into night. I always appreciated the peacefulness of it.

Boredom was a constant in my life. Killing was the only act that I had which would drive it away. A short man, round around the middle in an expensive, perfectly tailored suit exited the front door. I casually strode across the street. My distance behind my mark was enough that his instincts wouldn't kick in that he was being followed. Yet still close enough he was always in sight.

My mark walked to the parking garage down the block. I'd already scoped out his spot on a mid-level. And while it would've made more sense to wait for him there, a stranger hanging out around vehicles had the potential to draw attention.

The time of the act drew closer, but my heart didn't pick up speed. I subtly looked around and even nodded at a lady who passed me, her smile small and brief. It was that polite smile that always came with false politeness—just some societal expectation. I'd studied every visual, emotional cue —every microexpression. In order to blend, you need to be perceived as normal and respectable.

I slightly increased my pace when he turned the corner into the garage. His vanity worked in my favor because he took such pride in his middle-aged crisis sports car. He parked it on a nearly empty level. My steps echoed as I slipped inside and shot out my arm to catch the elevator door before it closed.

I chose the floor above his and reclined against the back wall of the elevator. He didn't spare me a glance or start in on the small talk so many people tried awkwardly to initiate. If they used security footage in the elevator, the brim of my cap concealed my face and the prosthetics I used softened my angler features. I'd padded my shoulders, chest, and waist, and probably added a twenty-pound illusion to my slender frame. The inserts in my shoes gave me another inch in height. I'd already scoped out the security protocol, and they only videoed entry and exit points.

The small ding signaled we'd reached his floor. He exited, and just as the door began to close, I stepped through the narrow space. I stopped as I let my gaze scan the dim interior. The lights didn't break the shadowed edges. A few cars were parked on the opposite side, and my mark's footsteps were the only ones I could hear. I bent my arm behind me to reach under the hem of my jacket, and everything inside me went still at the sound of steel on leather as I unsheathed my blade.

Even in the cavern of the garage, with practiced stealth, my steps barely made a sound. I mentally planned it out, saw it in its every step, from the grab to the second I pressed my blade to his throat. The last few steps, I jumped and placed my hand over his mouth, and his futile struggles were nothing against my strength. The cool edge of my knife against his throat instantly ceased his fighting, and I dragged him to the other side of his car. I kicked at the back of his knee, and he fell, and I released him.

He opened his mouth to beg and the corner of my mouth lifted into a cold smirk.

"You can have whatever you want. Here's my wallet."

He frantically dug the item from his back pocket and tried to offer it to me. When I didn't take it, he promised me everything from his car to whatever money I wanted.

"I have a hundred grand...it's yours."

"Do you think money solves everything?" I asked as I drew the lethal point down his rounded cheek and nearly gasped as the skin split. The thrill started to build, and the pleasure nearly had a shiver running the length of my body. He bit his lip to keep in his scream as I repeated on the other side.

Terror made people do odd things. When he could call out for help, he seemed frozen. I crouched down to put us at eye-level. I started picking the buttons from his shirt until the pale, smooth skin beneath was revealed.

"Do you know why you're going to die?"

His answer was a stuttered no, and I leaned in close, the stench of his sweat tickled my nose, and I nearly groaned at the way he flinched.

"You're about to find out." The strike was quick, and he fell backward, the sound of his head hitting the cement rang in every direction.

Then a scream and a cry for help jerked my head up. Fuck, a familiar man stared at me in horror, and as he fumbled to open his car door, he dropped his keys. I overtook him quickly and trapped his body between mine and the driver's door.

"Oh, how I wished you hadn't seen this," I whispered in his ear as I wrapped my arms around his neck in a submission hold. I compressed his carotid arteries. He clawed at my arm, but I felt the life ebbing from him, and when I could've held on longer and ended the complication he caused, I eased the pressure. He slumped to the ground at my feet, and as I reformulated my plans, I stowed both men in the car, my target in the trunk and Harrison in the front seat. I had a limited time frame until they'd come to and I needed to be at my destination. My car was stowed at a storage unit I rented on the other side of the city. I had my second parked in the garage at my cabin.

Both needed to die, I'd made it this far without detection, and I couldn't allow Harrison to keep living. He wasn't the first witness I'd done away with since I'd started this particular career path. Yet, I'd never known any of the others. It was too close to home.

I drove out of the garage and toward the city limits and beyond to the mountains and my sanctuary.

Minutes turned slowly into an hour. The banging in the truck alerted me to the fact my mark had come to, but Harrison, except for a few groans in his sleep, remained still beside me. He looked so peaceful. Unaware what I had in mind for him. I'd always wanted to play with him, and since he would die, there were no constraints on my actions. A few days of teaching him how pain could be pleasure, then kill him as I'd planned. This way I could find out if I was right about the sweetness and submissiveness the man kept hidden.

I'd researched him and memorized his routine. No one came into my life without me learning everything about them. He had no one left. His parents both deceased. No friends that I could find other than the employees of his favorite eating establishment. He lived a rather sad existence. If I didn't write his paycheck, I could dump his body anywhere, and it would just be another *John Doe*.

I cursed the whining of the engine as the car struggled to make it up the steep hill to my cabin. The place was purchased under an alias I'd created through a corporation long defunct. No mortgage and completely solar-powered from electricity to the water pump. At some point, I figured I'd need to retire, and this played a part in my plan. I broke into the small clearing, and the headlights illuminated the front door. The man in the trunk had stopped trying to escape fifteen minutes ago.

I made quick work of parking inside the garage, and I got Harrison in a fireman's carry to take him inside. I'd stow him in the cellar and decide what to do with him later. The stairs creaked under our combined weights, and with cold efficiency, I stripped him. The scent of musty, wet earth caused me to wrinkle my nose, and there was a definite chill in the air. I shackled his wrists and ankles, secured him to the far wall and tossed a blanket over him. I didn't spare him much study before I jogged upstairs to take care of my job.

The money was good, and with what I'd saved up over the last decade, I'd never have to work again. It wasn't the reason I took the job. No, I took it for the fact it was the one place I'd fit and where my skills were perfectly honed. In the living room, I removed my clothes and padding until I wore only my jeans, then kicked off my shoes beside the door.

Grass and damp soil teased the spaces between my toes and the soles of my feet as I descended the porch steps. I had a workroom off the garage that led to what I learned was a stone furnace used by blacksmiths. Cremating the body was easiest, and then only ashes need spreading. I squared my shoulders and widened my stance to strengthen my center of gravity. Then I opened the trunk. If I'd anticipated a fight, I was sorely mistaken because he lay curled in a shivering ball.

I dragged him from the cramped space, and he tried to dig in his heels, but I had him locked in the room and strapped to the work table in the center in no time. He had his eyes squeezed shut as if not looking at me would change his fate. It wouldn't.

I slapped his cheek, and as quickly as he looked at me, they were closed again. I straightened and moved to the counter with my tools laid out, shiny and pristine. I didn't always kill. Occasionally, I'd get a job where someone needed information.

"I find it interesting that you don't want to look at me. From what I heard, you love imparting secrets to law enforcement about what you've...witnessed." I chose a scalpel and turned to the table. "What should I remove first?" I forced my thumb into the side of his mouth and pushed the blade into his tongue. "Your tongue. Or maybe..."

I didn't warn before I held his head still and removed his eyelids. His screams were let free. No one lived any closer than a five-mile radius. "Now do you see me? Well, let us begin."

Chapter Four

HARRISON

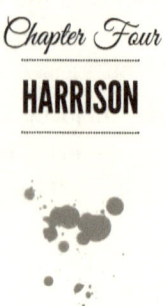

I groaned as I awakened and for the hundredth time remembered that I needed to get a new mattress. My back and shoulders were killing me. I tried to roll onto my back, and metal cut into my wrists. The pain brought me to full consciousness quickly enough to make me dizzy. A headache I didn't realize I had exploded painfully behind my eyes. My body prickled with chill bumps and realized I was bare except for a thin blanket tossed across my thighs. The room was completely dark, and I felt the dirt between my toes and under my ass as I tried to pull at the restraints around my wrists and ankles.

I screamed into the dark. Frantically searched for even a sliver of light. I tried to get my brain to function enough through the fear and disorientation to let me know what happened. When I shifted to my knees, I used my mass to deadweight and tried to break whatever had me trapped. It wasn't any use, and agony radiated outward from my shoulders as I felt them begin to pop.

To distract myself, I played out what I did remember. It was Saturday, and I'd had errands to run. All I could recollect was the meeting with the financial advisor who I was speaking with to cut the payments. Afterward, I'd felt defeated. I refused to file bankruptcy to take care of the rest of the medical debt, so I'd wanted something comforting and decided to treat myself to ease my depression. That overly expensive coffee was the end, and everything else was black or fuzzy.

I wasn't worth anything. No one would pay a ransom for me. I was corrupted code in the *Matrix*. Useless and easily erased. A part of the scenery no one ever noticed. Maybe I spent too much time watching TV and movies.

The boards above me creaked with slow steps, treating and returning as if the person paced.

"Help! Why am I here?" I bellowed at the top of my lungs at those ghostly steps, and then they receded again. The scrape of a heavy metal lock started to build my hope for the dimmest of lights. I hated the dark. A silly childhood phobia I'd never quite been able to get over. I imagined monstrous demons in the shadows. Their clawed hands reaching to drag me into them.

The planks of stairs gave eerily under lazy footsteps. I couldn't see anything. What I assumed was a nightlight in the room above didn't broach farther than the opened doorway. The stranger didn't say a word, and the dirt floor muffled where he'd stopped in what I assumed was a cellar or unfinished basement.

I counted clicks of a chain switch on an overhead light being pulled. At five, a bare bulb flared to life, and the sudden brightness forced my eyes closed as stars danced behind my lids as the pain in my head exploded. I forced them open and stared down at the ground. The soil was wet and my knees sunk into it. Shame heated my face at my completely naked form and caused me to try and cover myself, but I'd kicked the blanket too far away in my panic.

I quickly brought my gaze to the stranger and found him in the shadows beyond the circle of illumination. He was using a crimson-stained towel to wipe what looked like blood from his hands. His face was concealed behind a mask that covered all but his mouth and the lower right of his face, but the same substance on his hands looked as if was sprayed across that exposed skin.

"What am I doing here? Let me go, I don't know..."

The laugh that answered me was guttural and without emotion. "Now, boy, do you think begging will get you anywhere with me? You woke chained in my basement. Naked and alone."

I didn't recognize his voice, it was dangerous and barely above a whisper. His calmness strengthened my terror. I would understand anger, ranting, or a frenzied attack. As much reaction as the stranger showed, we could be conversing over coffee instead of me waking to find myself chained in his basement like a captive.

"But I'm no one." I hated the quiver in my words.

"That I won't deny."

"Then why..."

"I grow tired of your incessant questions. The only thing you need to be aware of is that you're mine to do with as I see fit. Are you ready to learn your rules?"

"Who are you?" I yelled in a high-pitched, cracking voice. "I just want to go home."

"Are you ready to learn your rules?"

I continued to plead with the stranger. My limbs were cramping and shaking with cold and hysteria. His voice didn't change—it remained flat and calm. It was that which terrified me the most. I could deal with death. Rules implied the stranger was going to keep me and what would he subject me to, and no one would think to look for me.

The urge to ask him once more was tempered by the fact I grew more chilled by the second.

"What do you want from me?"

"It's quite simple, follow the rules that I set. Now, are you ready to learn your rules?"

"Y-yes."

"Before I list your rules, let's discuss your punishment. For every infraction, you earn one lash, but in some cases, you will earn up to three for every rule broken."

I was so shocked by what he said that I didn't even protest what he was suggesting. Tears began to flow hot down my cold cheeks, wetting my short beard.

"You will call me sir when you address me, is that understood?"

"S-sir?" My thoughts were chaos, and all I could focus on was the punishments. *Lashes.* Did he mean from a whip? What had I done? Was this all a nightmare that I would eventually wake up from—maybe a night terror. I squeezed my eyes closed and mentally begged to wake up, but when I opened my eyes, he was still there—closer. I was eye-level with his belly, and I couldn't make myself lift my gaze higher than that.

"As I give you the rules, you will respond *yes, sir* after each. Tonight, you won't earn correction, but from tomorrow forward, you will earn lashes from my whip."

"Y-yes, s-sir." My free will seemed to slip away with those two simple words. They wouldn't mean the same thing to me ever again. A statement of respect now proof of my unwilling submission.

"Rule one...you will follow each order as given."

"Yes, sir."

"Rule two...you will thank me for each lash given."

My naturally shy nature fought with my will to survive. If I did what he asked, maybe he'd let me go. His appearance was hidden behind baggy clothes and a leather mask. I'd never be able to identify him.

"Do I need to repeat? Your hesitancy in the future will earn you one lash."

"Y-yes, no, you don't have to repeat. Yes, sir."

"Rule three...you will be ready to please me. If I tell you to suck my cock, you will do so. If I tell you to bend over and spread your cheeks, you will do so."

I dropped my chin to my chest. "I can't do that."

"Then you will earn lashes. Rule four...you must follow all instructions as given to earn rewards. We'll start off simple and rules will be added as I deem necessary."

"Y-yes, sir." They came too easily that time, barely a stutter. I wanted to go home. My life may be quiet and uneventful, but it was mine. "What are the rewards?"

"You will address me as sir. Each slip will earn you a lash."

"What are the rewards—sir?"

"You will earn clothing. A bed. Treats. You will earn the right to come upstairs. To sleep on the floor beside my bed. To sit at my feet. Tomorrow I will bring you a few items, and you'll begin your stay."

"Why are you doing this to me, sir? I don't know who you are."

"Why, boy, I'm doing it because I can."

I tilted my head back as he retreated and I watched as his arm seemed to rise in slow motion.

"No, please—please leave it on."

"What do I get in return for the kindness of leaving your light on?"

"I don't know, sir, please, I don't—"

I threw myself back against the wall as he undid his zipper and started to free his penis.

"Rewards are earned, boy. If you don't do something to show what a good boy you are, then why should sir give you something for free?"

I couldn't answer, and suddenly, just as it was when I woke up, the room was black. I followed his steps until his silhouette was visible for mere seconds before the door slammed. I stretched as far as I could from where I was secured to the roughhewn wall behind me and wrapped the scratchy blanket around me to ease the chill in the air. My bladder screamed for relief, and I mentally cursed myself for not asking to use the bathroom or for something to drink or eat. I could only assume it was late evening, maybe just hours before dawn.

My only comfort was that he wouldn't kill me—didn't seem as if he would—but what did he want with me? He didn't explain why he was doing this to me, and because he could, wasn't an answer. Where did he see me? Why did he decide I was the one he wanted to chain in his basement? The one he wanted to call him sir.

This wasn't a fantasy of mine. I didn't understand any of it. I'd watched porn, I knew about BDSM in theory, but this —this wasn't what I saw in those videos. Was I being groomed for something else? I wasn't the type to be kidnapped for those stories of human trafficking. It was always young men and women, teenagers. Did he want to break me just because I was bigger or manly appearing?

I was nothing of the sort. I curled into a fetal position and tucked the blanket beneath my chin. Out of all the happy places my brain could go for a moment of reprieve, it went to those silly dreams I had before I woke up here. The man who would come in and love me for me. He'd hold me and make love to me. He'd accept me with all my faults. Tears started to seep from beneath my lids again while I mourned the life I'd dreamed of and tried not to think about my new reality.

Chapter Five

COWEN

I had cooked breakfast and made coffee like I was normal that morning. Everything I did was out of necessity. I ate and drank because my body needed it to sustain me. Slept and exercised for the same reason. The requirements in my life were simple and biologically imperative. The food I consumed tasted as I assumed it should. I rarely contemplated or compared my existence.

Who said that I wasn't normal in an abnormal world? That violence wasn't the natural order of things. Unnatural death as population control.

I rinsed the last plate and placed it in the dish drain. Rinsed and dried the sink. I'd checked on my guest that morning, and he still slept.

Harrison's basic needs were requirements for his stay with me. I pivoted on my toes to study the tray of food and then glanced at a large duffel bag that contained the items I'd packed when I'd awakened. There was a roughly enclosed room in the corner of the cellar I assumed the original owners used as a pantry when the home was built. The door had long since disappeared. There was a spigot beside the entrance. He would be able to clean himself and get his own water, but I would provide food.

He wouldn't be in my care long. When his time came, and my boredom reappeared, I'd do away with him as I'd done all the rest. I was still unsure about the reason I wanted to keep him. I understood my compulsion to play with him. To absorb his pain for a momentary reprieve from my existence. I'd threatened him with the demand for a blowjob, but I had no intention of fucking him.

Experiencing emotion through the study of another was one of the few acts I found fascinating. I returned the mask to my face, securing the buckles at the back of my head. I took two measured steps and rearranged the items on the tray. The food was still warm from where I'd stored it in the oven. It was the same as I'd eaten, eggs, bacon, and toast. I picked up the tray and balanced it on one hand as I strode to the door. I slid the bolt lock aside and pushed the door open with my toes. I easily leaned down to grab the handles of the bag and straightened

The stairs strained under my slight weight. I'd used the cellar only on one other occasion. Most of my jobs were as an assassin, but there were certain times that my employer wanted information. That man had found himself chained to one of the support pillars. I hadn't cared about his basic needs. The interrogation took no more than twelve hours, and I'd left the bloody and broken man on a sidewalk as a warning.

I walked easily through the dark and crouched to place the items I held on the floor. The lantern would only require him to wind it up. I did so and then set it on one of the shelves on the right side of the little room.

"Hello?"

His voice was broken and slightly husky from sleep. I

didn't respond, just finished placing more blankets on the remaining shelf space along with books to keep him occupied. I spread a towel on the ground and laid my whip on top of it. I stroked the woven leather with the tips of my fingers. I couldn't remember the last time I'd removed it from its box, and I felt a brief thrill at the thought of using it.

Then I removed the last item from the bag. One I'd left last night to purchase for him. I straightened and placed it in my pocket. When I approached him, he cowered back to the wall. I didn't say a word as I released his cuffs from the chain secured to the wall.

He whimpered in pain as I jerked him to his feet with my hand fisted in his soft hair. I quickly had him secured to a pillar in the center of the cellar. He twisted his body to conceal his cock from me. His bulky frame was covered in thick, dark hair. His pubes were wild and untrimmed.

"Be still," I ordered as I gripped his hips and forced him back on the rough wood.

He refused to meet my gaze as I pulled the chain to turn on the bulb above his head. His body was stretched taut by his cuffs over the hook high enough to force him to stand on his toes. I studied him as I would an object. To me, he wasn't anything more than a possession—something to be used and discarded when it had served its purpose. I pinched the softness of his belly, spun him and squeezed his ass until he gave me another pain-filled sound. I measured the breadth of his back with the flats of my hands. He had a patch of hair in the hollow of his lower back and more on his shoulders.

I spun him back to face me. His face was red, and tears streamed down his cheeks. I frowned and felt my brows pull together. I raised my hand, stroked the wetness from one cheek and then brought my fingers to my mouth to lick the saltiness from the tips.

The groan that slipped from my throat took me by surprise. I dropped my arm to my side, and when I grabbed his cock, he tried to kick and attempted to swing away. I squeezed harder until he yelped.

"The more you fight me, the more I'll make you hurt. Am I understood?"

"Y-Yes, sir."

"Now, you are not to touch yourself without my permission. You are only allowed to touch your cock if it's to take a piss. From this moment on, I own it and every orgasm you have."

I could see the war raging in his eyes. His will to survive overshadowing his rage. It was there. The anger that said he'd attempt to hurt me the moment his hands were free. As easily as he gave into my orders, I had a feeling that maybe he wouldn't break as fast as I'd first anticipated.

With my left hand still secure around his cock, I reached into my pocket with my right to remove the cool metal. I only released his penis long enough to use the key to remove the lock and open the thickest ring. He didn't speak, simply stood there as I slipped his flaccid length into the device. I closed it trapping his cock and balls. I shivered at the whisper of the click as I secured the tiny lock. When I stepped back, I crossed my arms over my chest to admire the chastity device. His chest heaved as he tried to catch his breath. His head tipped all the way back to hide his expression from me.

"Look at me, boy."

I advanced on him, gripped the metal and jerked. His watery gaze met mine, but there was also defiance there.

"Boy, what did I tell you last night? What was rule number one?"

"I was to follow all orders, or I would earn punishment."

"Exactly." I spun him away from me. I ignored my whip for now. I spanked him with no mercy, his screams mixed with the sound of his flesh and metal hitting the beam. I didn't soothe or pause; I spanked until my handprint was red and swollen on his hairy ass cheeks.

"Do you like that, boy? Sir showing you the error of your ways?" I asked as I spread his cheeks and pushed my thumb to his tight, wrinkled hole. The muscles resisted the intrusion, and I shallowly worked him. I held his cheeks open as he tried to clench and spin away from my touch.

"No."

I turned him back around. His cock was soft inside the cage. His chest abraded from the beam. He even had scratches where the rough surface had broken the skin.

"Good. Your pain is all I want. Your pleasure is unimportant."

I left him there as I moved upstairs, washed my gloved hands, and then grabbed the small air mattress I'd prepared earlier. I ignored his presence as I finished getting his space ready. I gave him no more than he needed. The books were left over from a time I attempted to analyze my lack of sexual attraction and the depth of my emotional detachment.

I released him and drove him to his hands and knees. "Crawl."

He did as ordered, but I noticed his movements faltered, and I smacked his abused ass. The pain caused him to collapse, and with his wrists secured, he was unable to protect himself.

"I said crawl."

He moved quicker. An odd sensation prickled at my nape. It was that feeling I had when I was being watched. Although, that wasn't the case. There were sensors all over my property, and my system would've alerted me at the first step onto my land.

He surged forward into the small space and huddled against the wall.

"There's a spigot for water. There's a toilet." I pointed to a darkened corner where a tiny alcove was hidden. The bowl was cracked, and besides a single flush when I first moved in, I assumed it worked.

"Why are you doing this? I want to go home. Please, just, I won't tell anyone. I don't even know who you are."

Each word fell off his tongue with increasing desperation. They cracked with fear and frustration, if I felt anything, I might have had a moment of remorse. His tears and pleas didn't move me.

My brows drew tightly together behind the mask. What did I see him as except an object? The means for a fleeting break from routine. My cock remained soft and unmoved. Whatever I'd experienced at his pain was a muted thrill.

"This is your home now. When I am done with you, I will dispose of you as I see fit. If I'm feeling merciful, your death will be quick. Don't make me hurt you more than necessary. I will definitely enjoy it more than you. Eat and prepare...your first lesson begins after lunch. Do not wander any farther than the bottom step. Disobey, and you'll find yourself chained to the wall again."

I bent and picked up my whip, hung it from a hook in the doorway.

His gaze fixed on the coiled length of leather. As the light of the lantern faded, his eyes grew wide and frightened. I studied that expression until all was dark and I backed up, I turned and strode toward the overhead light. I turned it off and removed the bulb, my fingertips burned, yet I was as calm as always.

I longed to feel. To experience what others did. Maybe I wasn't human, but a demon as my parents accused me of being as I descended further into the nothingness. I didn't miss what I'd never felt. That's where my obsession had bloomed from. The fact that I didn't understand what it meant to be human.

As the bolt slid into place, my phone chimed from my office. It was the one I only used for my employer. He rarely used my services so close together, and even though I wanted to play with my new toy, I required something to soothe the beast who demanded I take a life. I'd do away with Harrison soon enough, but for now, I'd keep him. But for how long?

Chapter Six

HARRISON

fter my captor left me in the dark, I'd desperately searched for the lantern. My hands shook as I tried to figure out how it worked and didn't relax until I figured out that I needed to wind it up. Once the small room was filled with light, my panic eased. I knelt in the dirt and ate all the food on the tray.

I loved food. I liked to savor it and enjoy each bite, but my stomach was so empty it hurt. Was it only a day since my life was normal? Had I cursed myself contemplating how no one would even care if I disappeared? No one would even notice until I didn't show up to work tomorrow. Cowen barely tolerated my presence. He'd probably be relieved when my desk remained empty. I stumbled backward onto the mattress. I flinched at the pain that reminded me of the spanking. No one had ever put their hands on me. I couldn't help crying when he'd spread my cheeks and forced his thumb into my hole.

There was nothing sexual about what he'd done. His temperament hadn't changed. Even the sharp tone of his voice hadn't carried an ounce of sentiment. There was nothing there. And I wondered again why he wanted to keep me.

My gaze moved down my body over the hair covered rolls of my belly to the connected steel rings that encased my dick, and the thickest circle irritated the sensitive skin behind my sac. The tiny lock seemed fragile enough to break but as I pulled and twisted it, pain radiated outward from my groin. I was like an animal trapped. Restrained and forgotten, my captor held my life in his hands.

He'd made it quite clear that he'd kill me when I was no longer useful to him. I didn't want to die. There were so many things I wanted to accomplish. I didn't want to lose my virginity in this cellar to some insane stranger who only wanted my pain.

I crawled forward to get some water, it sputtered as I turned the metal tap, and I drank until my belly hurt. The shackles around my ankles made it impossible for me to walk safely and I didn't want to chance breaking the lantern if I fell.

I couldn't survive down here without something to push the shadows to a safe distance. I was long past the age of childish fears, but this was the only one I hadn't been able to shake. It seemed to take forever to find the toilet. I found the edge of dirty, cracked porcelain and realized there wasn't a seat. I struggled to my feet, the chain between the shackles only stretched shoulder width, and it took forever for me to figure out how to empty my bladder with my cock trapped.

I emptied my overly full bladder and sighed in relief. I was no less scared because he'd reluctantly given me lights and an under-inflated mattress, but I didn't care. Grown men scared of the dark, my fear humiliated me, but I couldn't get over it. My captor was at least attempting to keep me alive, but I didn't know for how long. What if he did all this to lull me into a false sense of security, and when I was comfortable, he'd snatch it all away.

I didn't know or understand what to do because he hadn't explained anything. All he'd done was imprison my cock in a cage with a lock. He wouldn't allow me clothes, but he'd given me a blanket to conceal myself. I tried hard to figure out what to do. *But what happens if I'm able to escape?* I couldn't see outside, and I could be anywhere in the city, and what if I'd slept longer? I could be in another country for all I knew.

On my way back to the tiny, dimly lit space, I stopped to wash my hands and face. A shiver moved down my body at the chill in the air. The air mattress compressed under my weight and I wrapped the blankets tightly around me. I remembered the food on the tray, classic breakfast, eggs, bacon, and toast, but all I could think about was had my captor poisoned it. Did he want to make me sick? Torture me more than he had already.

Would I have already started feeling sick? All the ways the man could hurt me came quickly to my mind. He'd warned of a first lesson after lunch, and my gaze went reluctantly to the whip the man had on a hook screwed into the right side of the doorway. Time passed with no sense of realness as I couldn't tell what it was like outside. No windows to show me the sun. I wanted to cry but didn't see how that was helpful. My captor had stroked the tears from my cheeks, brought his hand to his mouth, and almost seemed to savor the taste of them.

The stranger only wanted my pain, and I didn't see as if I had a choice. No one would look for me. Hadn't I thought about this before, my disappearance wouldn't cause a stir at all.

Locks disengaging echoed in the dimness and I hadn't

realized the lantern had died down. I backed into the corner, prepared to fight, but knew it wouldn't do any good.

The light shining upward cast my captor in frightening light, highlighting the unnatural planes of the mask the man wore. There was something familiar about the small glimpse of skin. I tried to place it, but the fear made my brain fuzzy.

"Are you ready for your first lesson?"

"Why...why are you doing this?"

"I already answered that question, boy, and I won't repeat myself," the man answered as he lifted his hand to pull down the whip.

A deadly calm seemed to come over my captor as the leather slithered through the man's slim, elegant hands that were encased in tight black leather. "Remove the blanket, stand and return to the support in the center of the room."

Every inch of my body shook as I did as he asked. The chill in the air had goosebumps rising and caused the hair to stand up on my arms. When I straightened, I used my hands to cover my crotch. Each step I took fought against my instinct to survive. He said he'd do away with me, and if he felt merciful, he'd make my death quick. As much as that should have terrified me, it brought me a sense of comfort that once he was done with me, he wouldn't make me suffer.

I yelped and covered my eyes as the single, naked bulb burned bright.

"Face the support and grab the hook. Do not remove your hands from it at any time or you will earn an extra lash."

My captor's voice turned deeper, almost what I assumed a lover would sound like.

"What are you going to do with me?"

"I'm going to teach you, boy, that pain is pleasure.

When I'm done, you will beg for each lash you receive in punishment."

I arched my back as he drew the hilt of the whip down the indent of my spine and then I felt his breath fan my ear. "You have to embrace pain to truly appreciate pleasure. For some of us, they are one and the same."

That he believed what he was saying was scarier than the inevitability of my death.

My captor pressed his clothed form fully to my back. The man was lean, but I felt the power in those muscles, and I cried out as strong fingers winched my head back. I closed my eyes at the burning sting on my scalp. The rough support abraded my skin—only the cage on my cock protected the tender skin. My big, hairy body was too on display, and I didn't want him to look at me.

Suddenly the heat and presence of him was gone, and the chilliness of the damp basement washed over me. I didn't dare turn around. I didn't want to see what was about to happen. I knew that was stupid. He was going to whip me and seeing would allow me to brace myself for the pain.

"Breathe, boy. I own every inch of you, and that includes your pain."

As soon as the last syllable slipped from his tongue, I felt the fire of the first kiss of the whip. Strangely, I flinched more at the crack of the leather than I did the first strike. I moved to wrap my arms around the support, hugging it tight and pressing my sweaty brow to the splintered surface. Each strike of the whip made me writhe and beg. I wanted the pain to stop. I felt the first trickles of blood down my back. It was a tickling sensation as it flowed over my ass— the backs of my thighs.

It wasn't as much as I'd assumed, as if just the tip of the whip grazed my back. The agony reached the point that a sort of numbness took over. The nerves had dead-ened under the exposure of overwhelming suffering. My vision was dimming at the edges, and my heart beat too fast, I cried out with each new lick of leather. I was posed on my tiptoes, and my thighs shook, I was on the edge of collapse.

I was granted a reprieve, and I screamed as his soft shirt felt like sandpaper on my abused back. "Good boy, you did better than I expected." His voice sounded almost...caring, and that was so unlike the mental picture I'd formed of him. I gritted my teeth as he drew his palm from my shoulder to hip. I was oversensitive and shoved myself harder into the beam.

"Easy, boy, you did so good. I've never seen someone so beautiful in the throes of their pain."

He was pressed close to my ass, and I felt no hardness behind the zipper of his slacks. It wasn't the first time I didn't notice a sexual response and my confusion grew. If he wasn't going to use my body, why was he keeping me there? Did the only thing he require of me was to hurt?

I gasped sharply as a single fingertip traced what felt like a split in the skin of my back and then he was gone. At his desertion, I collapsed to my knees in the dirt, and my adrenaline started to ebb away. Cold and pain became an intense maelstrom of sensation, my suffering was soul deep, and I became lost in it. It was as if I existed outside of my body—I was there but on the peripheral.

The pitiful whimper I pushed past my lips at the first touch of a tepid rag to my back brought me out of my thoughts. He whispered to me as he cleaned what I assumed were long, raw lines. I sat there in the dirt of the floor with my knees hugged to my chest. He continued to tend to my wounds, and then I sighed in relief as he smoothed a cream along the damage and left numbing relief in the wake of his oddly gentle touch.

I frowned as my confusion grew exponentially due to the contradictions my captor displayed. Cruel, yet caring, was that his plan? To keep me off-kilter so I wouldn't find my center—contemplate escape. The odd planes of his masked face stroked along my upper back, and I jerked at the softest kiss. His tenderness brought tears to my eyes. I felt as if I was losing myself. Could I succumb so soon and easily to a man who treated me as nothing more than a captive...a thing to hurt? Yet, the caring at the end of my punishment scared me more than my impending death. I could accept that he'd murder me, but what I couldn't was that he treated me with a gentleness that I'd craved for years. I couldn't protect against the depravity that was coming in the mask of caring; had I already given in? Was I already lost?

Chapter Seven

COWEN

I secured the house that morning when I left. Days had passed since I'd locked him in my basement. I knew the lack of light made it impossible to keep track of his time with me. Each lesson I gave him became sweeter as he took each lash with the most beautiful whimpers of pain and thanked me for each. Each second which passed made me want to keep him that much more. However, I knew I'd have to tie up the loose end that he represented. He was a weakness I couldn't afford.

Compartmentalizing my two lives had always been as simple as shutting off the part of my mind that didn't fit the situation. I looked at my life as a person with two personalities living separately from one another. Assassin me killing and/or torturing without remorse. Ending a life caused me no more contemplation than what I'd wear. Human me, my role I played to become a part of society, a thing barely remembered. Except for my success as a lawyer, nothing else about me would cause scrutiny.

I was a simple, plain man who carried himself with an aloofness. I always believed that if you played a role long enough, you could trick your brain into accepting it as fact. I could lie effortlessly.

I went through the motions of court, lunch meeting, and new client consultation at three, no one would look at me and think that I had my office assistant imprisoned in the cellar of my cabin.

Harrison had still slept when I'd left that morning. I placed food and a thermos of coffee on the shelf of his tiny closet. Why I'd stood there for moments I didn't have time to waste, only to watch him sleep, confused me nine hours later. There was something beautiful in the way he'd suffered under the lash of my whip. I'd used it on others in the past—ones I'd paid to endure my punishment. Masochist were easy enough to find, and they didn't require my body's response. They didn't require the kiss I'd placed to his upper back after I'd cleaned and tended his wounds. I questioned that single act far longer than necessary. A week later, I still wondered why.

The lust existed deep within myself as I'd observed the way he writhed, the beautiful whimpers of his pleas for me to cease. As always, my cock hadn't responded to the beauty in front of me. While celibacy was a choice, it wasn't altogether consensual.

My newest experiment was pornography. None of the many genres had done more for me than annoyed me with the exaggerated moans and vulgarity of sex talk. A scripted encounter without emotion. I found it lacked the elements I needed for study.

I shook my head to clear it of its newest contemplation and stared at the shelves. I'd studied Harrison for years. His obvious enjoyment of food. I knew the ones he savored the most. The scrunch of his face when he only brought a sandwich for lunch. I'd spent a long time peering into the bakery cases. I justified my care in picking his foods as I was charged with his keeping until the time that I saw fit to exterminate him. His comfort was my responsibility.

Glancing down, I cataloged the contents among the food basics. I'd never took care of anything in my life. My needs were minimal at best. I was probably thinner than was healthy, but eating was an unenjoyable chore. When I received no pleasure from anything, what was the point?

Irritation moved beneath my skin at the uselessness of my thought process, and I finished the rest of my shopping trip as quickly as possible. The politeness of the cashier made me snarl my nose, and her glance at me made her start packing my purchases quicker. I'd been away from Harrison for nearly ten hours. I'd kept a watch on him over the course of the day. I knew every move he'd made. I'd set up the cameras when I'd dropped off his food before I'd left the house.

I didn't understand this compulsion to simply watch him. While not classically so, he was a beautiful man. He was handling his captivity well. My second work phone vibrated gently in my pocket, and I paid for my purchases in cash. I was a man who left no more paper trail than necessary. I paid my taxes and made regular deposits, while my other money was sent to offshore accounts for my planned retirement.

Everything was planned down to the day I would leave this life behind and live anonymously in a country far away. My calculations told me I had another ten years, although I understood I was well past my life expectancy already. My body not only marred by the years of my self-harm, but also wounds of my trade. Knife and bullet wounds, a boss that I'd dispatched long ago in retaliation for attempting to blow me up, I'd literally given him my pound of flesh. Craters of missing pieces marred my side and back.

The last time I tried to take someone to my bed for a fuck even I could recognize the disgust they thought they hid before I noticed. Too thin and mangled to be pleasing to someone's eyes. The study of humanity became more interesting than humans themselves.

We were a demented, cruel people, although there was a minority of our species that seemed worthy of redemption. However, I didn't know many of them, the portion of the species I dealt with daily deserved whatever punishment they received.

I stowed my purchases in my trunk and leisurely made my way to the driver's side door. As always, I memorized my surroundings and the people that took up a portion of the scenery. I knew when I returned home that I could pick out every detail down to how many breaths a person took. Remembering everything kept me alive.

Once seated in my car, I checked the message on my secondary phone. Rarely did I receive jobs only a few weeks apart. A month or two would elapse in order for the heat to die down, or in certain cases, for a case to go cold. My service included a cremation of the person, unless my employer used the victim as a warning to enemies. I'd burned my last assignment down to ash and scattered them over a two-mile stretch of gravel road.

The drive to the park for me to pick up the new job packet took me away from my plans of returning home. I kept to my typical routine of sitting on the bench and staring out over the water. My two personalities warring for dominance. Routine kept me centered. I hadn't taken a life outside of my assignments in years, but my steely control was slipping. Soon I would have to do away with Harrison.

I'd make his death quick. Yet he'd cause me to break my rule, no civilian deaths. He's someone who'd be missed even if it was only as a regular who hadn't returned.

I anticipated the questions that would arise when they realized I hadn't reported my employee missing. Lying was second nature, employees left jobs all the time, and I pushed the thought aside.

On my way out of the city, I made several wrong turns. When I felt it safe to assume no one was following me, I headed to my cabin. The supplies I'd left him wouldn't last much longer unless he'd decided to conserve them in the event that I wouldn't feed him regularly. He was a big man, but confined as he was, he wouldn't burn the calories he would with regular activity.

I'd feed my guest and then study the details of the file and start to plan the job. The nuances of the planning stage invigorated me, and it was almost as if it amounted to foreplay. Anticipation building slowly to the climax—the killing. Those were the details I wouldn't rush. The act of killing was the ultimate power. A stranger at my mercy begging for their life. Even through the futility of their pathetic pleas, human nature urged a person to survive.

How could I give them something that I was unsure I could even feel?

Mercy, is that what made me spare Harrison's life? Did I feel something deeper than the visceral nature of my preparations to end his life? I was unsure of a lot in my existence lately. Almost four decades of careful study and mimicking the fickleness of human sentiment hadn't readied me for my unwillingness to do away with one useless human.

Our Earth slowly died with the increase in Global Warming. Crop failures. Malnutrition killing thousands a day. Mother nature was the most prolific serial killer in human history. Humans were no more important than a single speck of sand. Organisms to die out during the next great epoch. None of us were worthy of the space we occupied, yet in our arrogance, we placed ourselves at the top of the food chain. My life was measured in the lives I took and not in the days which passed. I didn't long for the permanence of leaving a legacy behind. As I'd always believed I live on borrowed time. I was nothing more than a loose end that would be tied up in a neat package. Buried in an unmarked grave. A feast for worms. I needed no accolades or a person missing me because it was meaningless when you were alone in the darkness—rotting cell by cell. When my time was up, nothing existed beyond that, and I didn't require some foolish person to mourn when I wasn't worth the emotional expense of bereavement and tears.

Chapter Eight
HARRISON

I attempted to twist my body far enough to see the newest damage to my back. While sore it wasn't painful, only a few spots made me scream in agony when they touched the wall, or I rolled onto my back. I'd tried to clean up as best as I could with the freezing water coming from the spigot. The stench of my unwashed body sickened me. Being hairy, I'd always taken great care with myself.

My captor had left me a tray that consisted of what I could assume were two meals, and there were a few snacks as well. I attempted to count my time there by the trays he left. But what if he didn't feed me every day? After his lessons, I had a tendency to sleep for hours, maybe a full day. I was so tired afterward that I didn't know what reality and time were anymore.

I savored the coffee. My caffeine headache made my head throb as I'd tried to fall asleep. While I was sure he fed me on a regular basis, I'd saved the prepackaged snack bars and fruit just in case. I stowed them away under the edge of my airbed.

I tried not to think of how long he'd kept me so far, or the fact that he was quite clear that he was going to murder me. He claimed he'd be merciful and make it quick. Yet, what happened if I angered him and he left me to starve to death down here? I was sure I'd read somewhere that a person could live for weeks without food depending on body fat and I had plenty of that. Water was another thing altogether, but unless somehow, he turned off the water to the house, I had a fresh supply to stay hydrated.

All the cruel things he could do to me played in my head. And I realized I'd watched too many true crime shows. My mind went darker with each scenario. The punishment I'd received confused me though. The praise had thrown me off, and I had yet to recover. His body hadn't responded to the pain he'd inflicted, but hadn't he clearly told me that all he wanted was my pain? I assumed he'd force me at some point. Although after whipping me, he hadn't seemed to react at all to what he'd done.

I stiffened in my crouch as I hugged the thermos to my chest as footsteps echoed on the floor above. The few sips of coffee that remained were for later. I followed his movements from what I assumed was one room to the next, staring at the spots where he briefly paused. A shiver worked through me, and I promptly wondered if he would give me clothes. It perplexed me why a stranger would want to keep me, and I went over the details of his face exposed by his mask, the thinness of his frame, and tried to remember if I knew him somehow.

The hours I was left alone, I planned an impossible escape. Could I overpower him in some way? I was a big guy but in no way did that mean I could defend myself. As slender as he was, he hadn't appeared to have any issue with controlling me. I knew it was mostly my terror that kept me confined there. I'd almost tried earlier, I spent long moments at the bottom of the stairs and focused on the light beneath the base of the door.

The only thing I could think was he was up there, waiting for me to make a move and finally give him the excuse to kill me. Silence didn't mean he left the house. All I could do was watch the unbroken line of light. At one point, I'd placed my foot on the bottom step and cringed as it creaked beneath my weight. I'd immediately brought it back to the dirt of the cellar floor.

In my boredom, I'd carried my lantern around and searched through boxes for items that might have proved useful. The contents were musty and some discolored with mold—no clothes or weapons. I did find a few water-stained romances that appeared to be from the eighties. I'd placed them on the shelf with the books he'd provided. I loved to read but hadn't relaxed enough to attempt to check out what he'd given me.

Minutes crept by and then I heard water running through the pipes. My stomach began to rumble with the first stirrings of hunger, and I assumed it was around dinner-time. I needed to devise a way to track my time since I'd became conscious. I was still leery if I was still in the city or not. While the windowless room made it impossible, I still thought I should hear some noises. Horns honking in traffic. Loud voices coming from the streets. Yet I heard nothing but silence only broken by the flow of water through pipes, sometimes my heartbeat as it increased with panic as the lantern dimmed.

Like the food, I didn't want to overuse my only source of light since he removed the overhead bulb each time he left. I was growing weary of worrying and wondered how lost I'd become when my hope disappeared. The locks at the top of the steps clicked, and I used my heels to move me backward until my body pushed flush to the wall. I peeked through the small spaces between the slats of the makeshift storage closet and only saw his outline from the light drifting down the stairs. Clutching the blanket tightly around myself, I jerked as he screwed in the bulb.

I squinted at the sudden brightness. He looked elegant in all black. It highlighted his slender frame, but my gaze locked on the tray he had balanced on one hand. I never looked away from the food steaming, and I frown as he lowered to place it on the ground.

"Hold out your hands."

I did so hoping that meant he intended to remove my wrist restraints. The tender skin was raw from the constant abrasion of the unforgiving metal. A tiny sound of relief left me as he unlocked first one wrist then the other.

"Eat."

It was a single order, and then he was gone with the empty tray. I didn't hesitate—it was one of my favorite meals. Meatloaf, mashed potatoes, and I wasn't even going to turn my nose up at the brussel sprouts. All I was given was a spoon. I ignored the movement outside my enclosure as I finished eating. As soon as I took my last bite, he returned, and I backed up to put a safe distance between us.

He entered my space and gripped my hair. His surprising strength forced me to my feet. I tried to catch the blanket I used to conceal myself, but it fell to the floor. As I was led to the outer room, I noticed the large mat on the floor. A bar of soap, shampoo and a bucket of water sat atop it. He roughly released my hair, and I stumbled, using my hands to cover my crotch. He wore black leather gloves, and he lowered himself to a chair he'd placed nearby.

"Wash." His voice was low and harsh.

I looked into the bucket to find a cup.

"Boy, I don't like to repeat myself." He said nothing else, and he was on his feet, he surged across the short space that separated us. With his hand fisted in my hair, he made me bend over. The first slap of his hand shocked me, but the second ruthlessly pulled me out of my surprise. I cried out as he spanked one cheek, then the other, repeating until I was attempting to get away. One minute he punished me and the next I was there bent over with him once more calmly seated.

"Wash. You definitely don't want me to do it."

I started to kneel to wet my hair and body with the cup.

"No, I want to see every inch of you. Keep your back to me as you bend over to wash your hair."

Humiliation caused my body to flush at what he meant. The entire time I washed my hair, I was aware of my ass cheeks on display, my balls hanging low, and I didn't dare look in his direction. I tried to block him out, enjoy the feeling of hair free of sweat and dirt. It took three cups of water to rinse the lather from my wavy hair. I took a deep breath as I used the cup to wet my body. I rubbed the soap between my hands, and the scent was musky and masculine, not some off-brand from the local discount shop.

I ran my hands over my chest, and just as I was about to stroke my hands lower to take care of my groin, he ordered, "I said I wanted to see. Must I punish you again?"

"No-no," I stuttered.

My ass was sore and on fire, the hot water wasn't soothing the pain. I didn't want another spanking. At least when I had to endure the lashes from his whip, he didn't touch me. I didn't want his hands on me. I quickly turned and scrubbed my cock and balls, taking care not to linger.

"Slower."

I stared at him to find him watching me. His legs crossed and his hands were folded over his lap. I continued to wash and rinse until my front was as clean as I could get it bathing with a cup and bucket. When I turned, I contorted trying to wash as much of my back as I could reach, feeling the welts that remained from my whipping. I soaped my hands again and hesitated when I reached my ass.

"Bend over, hold your cheeks apart and stay that way until I say so."

I did as ordered, but I was so nervous I was in danger of losing my dinner. I breathed in through my nose and out through my mouth, counting each inhale and exhale to eight, then seven. By the time I reached two, I was calmer.

"Has anyone ever fucked you before, boy?"

"No."

"Use a finger to fuck your ass."

I must have paused too long.

"Must I repeat myself?"

I thrust a single soapy finger past the tight rim of my hole.

"Deeper until you find your gland. Then I want you to stroke over it."

I swallowed around the returning lump in my throat as I did what he asked. I hated him. I tightened around my finger as a zing of pleasure traveled my spine, and I clenched my thighs. Shame infused my being as my cock painfully hardened in the ungiving metal of the cage.

"Finish washing. I think we're done with your lesson tonight."

I pulled my fingers from my body and rinsed the soap without hesitation. I straightened and shivered as the water began to turn chilly on my body. Suddenly I wished for my blanket. I stepped back as he approached me with a towel. His touch was impersonal as he briskly dried me.

"You smell like me now."

I lifted my gaze to his face as he spoke and the softness of his tone shocked me. His moods shifted so quickly I couldn't keep up. One minute he was humiliating me and the next he almost seemed to care. My arms were pinned to my side as he used the oversized towel to dry my back. His face was so close to mine that his leather-covered cheek nearly brushed mine. The differences in our sizes was noticeable as it appeared that I was a few inches taller than him and fifty pounds heavier. He was lean yet strong.

"Stay, I have a reward for you."

I was dizzy with another shift. He removed the items I used to bathe and only left the plastic mat I stood on. Why was I just standing there? The door to what looked like the kitchen stood open and I watched him as he moved around the tidy, brightly lit room. If I could knock him off balance, just take him by surprise, I could make a run for it. Yet I just stood there as he ordered. Other than the whipping and spanking, he hadn't made a move to touch me inappropriately since I'd awakened. His body didn't seem to respond at all. The only thing that worried me was the fact that he found no need to assault me sexually. All he wanted was me to suffer, and then he'd kill me.

Dying wasn't something I wanted, yes, I found my life empty, but I was in no hurry to end it. If I could just do as he asked, maybe when the time came, he wouldn't kill me. I could take the pain. I just had to make sure I kept his interest—no matter what that took.

When I left the house hours before to make the trip into one of the more exclusive neighborhoods, I analyzed the event from a few days before. While I'd seen Harrison naked, I hadn't taken the time to study him. While he was soft and didn't have an overabundance of muscle, I'd enjoyed the way he looked. My body was naturally devoid of hair except for the sparse hair at the base of my penis. The excessive hair on his chest, ass, and legs was pleasant to look at, and the thick bush around his cock was springy and soft. I remembered the feel of it when I'd secured his chastity device.

I hadn't planned to touch him when I ordered him to bathe, but I couldn't allow him to disobey my commands. Spanking him was so different from the times I'd whipped him. His ass soft and shook under the impact of my hand. My hand sank into the lush curves. I shook my head as I brought my attention back to my task at hand.

It was just my next step of stripping him of his body autonomy. He needed to learn that his body no longer belonged to him—that it was mine alone. Whatever I wanted to do to him was my prerogative. He would submit without thought. What I wanted I'd get, and the sooner he realized that, his life with me would become easier. The last few days, I did nothing more than make sure he was fed.

In those hours I observed him through the camera I had placed, I realized that I couldn't do away with him. I didn't understand when killing him was marked off as an option. In order to keep him, I needed to break him. I needed to make sure that he learned his only reason for living would be by making me happy.

Yet, I also found myself growing attached to him. I thought about him as I performed my daily tasks at work or simply when I laid in bed at night before I forced my body to rest. I hadn't slept more than a few hours a night in my life. At one point, I'd imagined all the scenarios I'd found intriguing when I moved him upstairs and had him sleeping beside my bed.

I also worried about how I would deal with another human in my space. I barely tolerated my own company. I rarely spoke for the fact that the tone annoyed me.

Thinking of him was dangerous and a distraction I didn't need. I could study the oddness of my reactions to him later. I stretched out in the high grass on my stomach.

I set up on a deserted road that ran along the back of my mark's home. The LED display of my watch flashed the time when I pressed a button on the side. It was almost one a.m., and my mark was having drinks with a scantily clad woman. I imagined the conversation going on between the two. The man's hand was tucked between the woman's thin thighs, and from her expression, she wasn't unwilling to receive his attentions.

My mark set his drink aside, and he dropped to his knees between her spread legs. His hands pushed up the cups of her bikini top to expose firm breasts, and she threw her head back as the man squeezed them. She threw her legs over his shoulders as he ate her pussy. I grew bored with the display.

Sex was a biological imperative to continue the human race. It was a desire some humans had to form a connection with another being on a physical level. As I'd never experienced pleasure during my limited experiments, I saw the act as completely unnecessary.

It would be easy enough to take him out as his female companion occupied him, but I had only received payment for the one kill. Unless she posed an inconvenience, I couldn't justify her elimination. I'd parked my vehicle a mile away and laid in the shrubbery that lined the abandoned road. When I'd staked it out a few days before, I hadn't noticed any fresh tracks in the dirt.

A high-pitched squeal moved along the breeze as my mark's companion reached orgasm. I rolled my eyes as the man pushed his swimming trunks over his ass and I stared down my scope. His head was beside hers. I slowly inhaled, and as I exhaled, I squeezed the trigger. Through the scope I watched my mark's head explode. Brain matter covered her face as the silent, horrified expression turned into a scream.

I calmly stood and slung my rifle over my shoulder. I would melt down the weapon as soon as I returned home. Not only did the furnace do away with the bodies I was contracted to dispose of, but it also served well to destroy other evidence. I made the leisurely hike back to my vehicle, stowed my weapon in the trunk, and got in the driver's seat. I turned on the scanner to monitor police channels.

The reciting of a familiar address made me pay closer attention. It wasn't for the location of the man I'd just killed, but Harrison's. Suspicious disappearance. A nine-one-one call was made for mail piling up. There was no mention of foul play. That was a complication I didn't need, but one that I'd seen coming. Sooner or later, I figured something would bring his disappearance to the attention of the cops.

I direct deposited Harrison's last paycheck for a full week, doctoring my payroll software that he'd clocked in and out on Monday and Tuesday. That would have him missing for only a few days without being accounted for. I'd driven by his house and didn't see his mail piling up.

The trip home didn't take long as my mark lived on the edge of the city. I made quick work of placing my rifle and my clothes in the furnace. I stoked the embers with an iron bar until the remnants of wood caught, then I placed fresh wood on top. It didn't take long for the seasoned wood to ignite. I strode barefoot across the yard and entered the house. I'd left long after I'd fed Harrison. Entering my office, I slipped behind my desk and sat naked in my leather chair. When I woke my computer, the cameras were the first thing I saw.

He was curled up in the middle of his mattress. I noticed that it was slowly losing air and I would need to take care of that tomorrow after I returned from work. I already anticipated a visit from the police as my office was Harrison's last known place of employment.

I felt none of the concern I probably should have when it came to a visit from law enforcement. I worked with them on quite a few occasions, mostly questioning them on the stand as I defended my clients, but we had a good rapport. I learned that if you treated someone with respect, you were more likely to be thought of with less suspicion. I'd made it almost forty years without a criminal record. Even in my teens, I was above reproach. They hadn't even investigated my parents' death, and after the age of sixteen, I hadn't repeated my therapy experience. Any tapes and transcripts had ended up burned right along with the doctor's body.

If I knew nothing in life, I knew how to dispose of evidence.

The shifting of Harrison's form made me focus and zoom in the camera a bit more. His blanket shifted and rested low across his hips. I traced the curve of his belly with my gaze. I pulled the memory of him bare in front of me as he bathed and wrapped my hand around my semi-erection. Stroking the length, I assumed men would be ashamed of the fact their dicks wouldn't get hard, but my flaccid length was just a way of life.

Maybe my impotence was about my inability to connect to another person on a human level. My emotional detach-ment the reason I couldn't sustain an erection long enough to enjoy the act. The inflicting of pain was the only sensa-tion that even made my body respond, but the moment I was done with the punishment, it was nothing.

I released my cock and got up to head to the kitchen for a glass of water before bed. I needed to continue Harrison's lessons. I couldn't allow his comfort to grow until he was unafraid of the death that I'd promised him. Yes, I was no longer killing him, but that didn't mean he needed to know about it. After I got the cops to move in a different direction, I would double my efforts.

I made a list of new purchases I'd need to make in order to move forward. I paused in front of the basement door as I downed the glass of ice-cold water. After I slept and took care of my work day, I had a weekend to keep him on edge.

Pain and pleasure, I needed him to be unsure of what came next. Reward or punishment, or could they be one and the same?

I felt invigorated by my new plan and how pretty my boy would be when he finally broke.

He'd awakened me by flipping me off my mattress. I'd blinked my sleep-blurred eyes as I had tried to figure out what was going on, and then I'd realized he'd exposed the snacks I'd hidden beneath my uncomfortable bed. It had steadily lost air over the last few days until I'd sunk to the hard floor. When I realized he was taking in the contraband, I'd thrown my blanket over them. His mouth had hardened, and he'd grunted as he filled my bed. Without another word, he'd tossed it at me and motioned to my daily allotment of food that would last me until he returned.

I was concerned by the fact he hadn't spoken to me. He used his words sparingly. No more than just orders. I'd only decided the day before to make myself useful. While I feared what he planned for me, his silence made it worse. Would he have inflated my bed if today was the day? He did appear the type to be nice before he slit my throat.

Lost in my thoughts, I didn't realize he was gone until I heard the basement door slam upstairs. I stared at the ceiling following his sure, even steps. Once I was positive that he was gone, I straightened my space up and stood to go to the bathroom. I still didn't like the shadows or the oppressive darkness of the tiny room.

I'd found a routine in my new reality. Bathroom, cleaning with the ice-cold water and then having my breakfast. I made sure to add the wrapped snack to the growing pile. I didn't know if I'd need them now that I feared he was ready to get rid of me. Maybe he was readying the space for his next captive.

I slowly ate my breakfast, today he served me waffles and not those frozen ones either. I enjoyed my food, but there was a new addition to the tray. A box with a note that read *don't open until ordered*.

He seemed too calm to have never attempted this before. I shifted to lie down on the mattress and stared up at the wood beams. The cock cage irritated my balls, and I grew tired of it. It wasn't as if I had felt a normal arousal since he'd locked me in here, but I didn't like the punishment. But wasn't that the point? He wanted to make sure I obeyed.

I hated feeling as if I was an unruly child. I didn't like being made to bathe in front of him. I still shifted uncomfortably remembering him watching me play with my ass. No one had ever witnessed me doing anything of the sort. I was always the chunky, unpopular boy, and while I'd kissed —did all the usual make out stuff—I'd never been to bed with a man.

When I imagined my first time, I'd never pictured I'd be locked in a basement/cellar and forced to expose myself to a man who didn't even seem to respond to the things he did to me. Wasn't that one of the first things I'd assumed when I'd awakened here? Terrified of being forced into sex, raped at a stranger's whim. I tugged the blanket higher on my chest to keep out the chill.

"Remove the blanket."

I jumped and pressed my back to the wall as an echoing voice came from the darkness. I'd heard him leave. The door had slammed.

How did I not realize that he watched me? He left for long stretches of time as if going to a regular job. He did mention that if I tried to escape, he'd know. I could've tried to escape a dozen times by now. Why hadn't I?

"Pick up the box. Stretch out on your back without the blanket."

I did as he asked only because I had a feeling my next punishment would be worse. I lay there hating the feeling of being exposed.

"Open the box."

He didn't waste his words, and I wondered if I'd met him before. The mask and the short sentences spoken in a low voice—almost a whisper. I swallowed around the lump in my throat as I opened the box and everything in me stopped. A massive dildo rested in the box beside a bottle of lube. I didn't care how much lube I used...this was going to hurt. It was twice that of my own toys.

"Fuck yourself—now."

I opened my mouth to argue as I stared at it and I thought he couldn't humiliate me more than he had when he'd watched me clean myself. My cock couldn't harden in the cage that trapped it. I could pretend I was alone in my bed and play out my favorite fantasy.

I flipped the top of the lube, slicked my fingers and closed my eyes. I made myself comfortable and brought my legs to my chest; the shackles around my ankles making it awkward. I reached past the curve of my belly and smoothed the slick around my hairy hole. With my free hand, I cupped my nuts and lifted them. At the slow thrust of one finger inside my hole, I mentally played out my recent favorite.

Cowen came up behind me in the office, and he placed his forehead between my shoulder blades. I loved that the smaller man liked my bigger body. A moan slipped past my lips, and I bit my lip before another one could escape. I pictured I moved my hands to take his hips. He never made me feel clumsy and unattractive, and he wouldn't assume I was a top because of my size. Just as I readied myself for my toys, I added another finger.

I ignored that my captor watched me on camera, but I couldn't ignore the discomfort as my dick started to harden inside the restrictive metal. Stopping wasn't an option. I knew what he'd do to me when he got home. I didn't carry fond memories of his whip licking over my back and backside.

"On your hands and knees with your ass to the entry."

I cursed as his brusque voice intruded, but again I did as he asked.

"Enough playing, slick your new toy and fuck yourself."

I wanted to protest and tell him I wasn't ready, but he didn't care. He wanted to humiliate me, and I wondered if he more than watched me—did he film me? Would there be evidence long after I left this basement? Would it matter if I was dead? Maybe that was the game? He imprisoned me for others to pay to watch him humiliate me—abuse me.

I kept swallowing as nausea built from the nerves anticipating the pain. I straightened only long enough to slick the long, thick dildo, it had to be ten inches, and my thumb and forefinger didn't meet. The lube I used was excessive, but I was relieved that he allowed me even that small amount of comfort. Awkwardly I held the base, my hand and the toy almost too slick for me to hold.

My teeth ground together at the intense burn and pain, whatever hard-on I'd had disappeared in that flash of pain. I whimpered in agony as the fat head popped past my rim. Sweat beaded my skin, thighs shaking as my body rejected the intrusion and the head slipped back out. I screamed, and my back arched as I forced it a few inches inside. I was panting and dripping sweat, as I shallowly fucked myself, trying to take another inch with each push.

I was in agony as the base met my ass. I was stretched so tight I couldn't even think about moving it. My body needed time to adjust, but I was sure my captor's patience was nearing an end. He'd bark his next order at any time. I was afraid to move a fraction of an inch.

"Must I repeat myself, your slowness has earned you ten lashes, would you care to add?"

"N-no."

"Do it. You're so pretty when you whimper."

My captor's voice softened just as it had the first night that he'd whipped me. Almost caring, as if what he was doing to me was normal. And who was I to say that I wasn't just one in a long line of captives.

I lost myself in my thoughts as I did what he ordered. My involuntary whines grew louder as I realized no amount of lube would make this comfortable. A twinge built in my shoulder and back at the odd angle and I tried to shift to make it easier, but nothing I did helped. I fucked myself as hard as possible figuring he'd grow bored sooner rather than later, then something terrible happened. The constant slide of the veined length over my gland started to loosen my hole, and my cock started to harden painfully inside its restraint.

I was horrified by the reaction of my body at the unwanted pleasure and the harder my dick became, the more the metal pinched. I couldn't come without stimulation, but I worked the dildo just so it constantly hit my gland. No longer was I whimpering and an image of me as if I was outside my body formed. Cowen's slender body was behind me. I was no longer filled with something fake—an instrument of my humiliation—it was Cowen taking me. Long powerful strokes, I swore I could almost hear the sounds of his grunts and the way his hips met my ass.

He was whispering to me. Dirty things. Telling me how much he loved my ass. It was his cock and his voice—my captor was no longer observing me as he would a rat trapped in a maze.

"That's enough."

The anger in the voice took me by surprise, and I froze with the dildo buried deep. My captor never spoke in anything other than a smooth, calm voice, but sometimes it contained a sharpness as it did when he whipped and spanked me. Although, never something that sounded on the verge of rage.

"Good boy. For doing as I asked, I will spare you punishment."

I waited long minutes on my knees, braced on one hand as I waited for another order, but it never came. Hard-on long gone and I winced as I started to remove the toy, thankful for the relief.

"No, you will sit on your bed with the toy in until I tell you otherwise."

I played his words over in my head. He wanted me to keep the thing in me. I was sore and raw from the size and insufficient slick. I started to remove it again.

"Do you like the lick of my whip?"

"N-no, sir."

"Do as I say. I will be watching, boy. I know every move you make."

I spun and sat down too quickly, and a twinge went through my stomach as the toy went in deeper. I hadn't cried nearly as much as I thought I should, but at that moment, I felt the tremble of my lower lip. A thought struck me, and I was terrified by it, would death be so bad?

Chapter Eleven

COWEN

"When is the last time you saw Mr. Clapton, Mr. Kingsley," The infuriating man asked for a second time since he entered my office. As if he was going to make me slip up on my story.

The big, barrel-chested detective jotted notes in a small notebook, then started watching me from under his bushy brows. He was almost the cliché of a grizzled detective. They'd shown up just as I knew they would. I had just ordered my boy to keep his new toy buried in his ass, and I planned for him to keep it there until I removed it. Having my scene with my boy interrupted had made me less affable to his presence. The detective was ruining my plans for the evening. If there was one thing I hated more than anything it was a disruption to my routine.

It had already taken several days to adjust to taking care of my guest permanently. If Harrison was at my mercy or not, I wasn't willing for him to die due to my neglect.

I concealed my deep breath and tried to control my irritation. "He left my office at five as always. I'm a stickler for my schedule, Tuesday, three weeks ago."

"Why didn't you report him missing?"

Even if I wasn't currently aware of where Harrison was, it would never have occurred to me to notify authorities over a person not showing up.

"He's my employee...why would I be concerned?"

"He's worked for you for"—he flipped through pages, and I was annoyed he'd forgotten a detail—"three years. Has he missed a day in that time?"

"He's taken the usual sick days which he was upset when I thoroughly rebuked him for his insubordination."

I felt the odd, uncomfortable pull in my cheeks as I attempted a smile. From his expression, the man didn't like me, and while I didn't care, I'd prefer if I didn't have to spend further time in his company.

"Does he have any friends? Maybe he mentioned a...partner."

Partner was pushed like a curse between compressed lips.

"His personal life or his sexuality is of no concern to me. As long as he did his job up to my standards, I didn't interact with him."

"Is that how you usually treat your employees?"

"He's only my second one. His predecessor was with me since I opened the office nearly fifteen years ago. She was irreplaceable."

She'd excelled as my office manager. Not only did she do her job as I required, but she rarely spoke of anything other than work-related subjects. When she retired, I realized how difficult it was to find a person such as herself. She was one of the only people I hadn't thought about killing once. She had a ruthlessness about her that I had greatly respected.

"Can we check his computer and desk?"

"I will have to ask that you refrain from accessing client files, that would be a breach of attorney/client privilege, but I see no issue with checking his search history and such. I restricted his use of the computer for personal emails or searches, but that doesn't mean he didn't."

"We'll send one of Computer Crime guys over the go through his desktop."

"Do you have a time so that I can arrange to be here? I'd leave the door open, but it's not the safest neighborhood, and I'll be out of the office for the weekend."

"The number you gave me earlier, is that the best one to reach you? I'll have them give you a call later or in the morning."

"Yes, that's my personal phone. I have problems with insomnia, but if I don't answer, they're welcome to leave a message."

"If you hear from Mr. Clapton, please keep us updated."

"Of course." I stood and steeled myself as I extended my arm across the desk to shake the man's hand. I tried not to grimace at the cool, clamminess of his skin. I slowly released the offending object.

We exchanged unnecessary pleasantries, and I let out a heavy relieved sigh as I closed the door behind the man. I was a half hour past the usual time I headed home. I gathered the items I would need for the weekend and adjusted my schedule to reflect the fact I would need to come to the office tomorrow for them to check Harrison's computer. Until then, it was time to confuse my boy more. I required him to question, and the more his confusion grew, the less chance he'd brace himself for my next move.

I needed to intensify his training in order to teach him that I owned him. I'd always assumed that if I ever found someone to keep, which I found naive, that I'd need to build a sense of trust. While I'd studied BDSM, and my urges seemed to lean toward sadistic, I didn't altogether see myself as a Master or Sir. In order to make Harrison mine, I'd have to adjust my thinking to the safe, sane and consensual mandate.

Would I be able to teach him to submit to my punishments and gain his trust?

My irritation grew with my confusion at my thought process. My drive home was riddled with mental contemplations of odd musings. I'd paid people well over the years to let me whip them or to watch them fuck themselves as my body wouldn't allow me to do it. I could remember a handful of times that I attempted to fuck, and in the end, I accepted my impotence and adapted. In my younger days, I'd masturbated as other boys had, but I found the pleasure that I received from it minimal at best.

My body and brain were broken, I accepted and didn't ponder, but when I'd watched Harrison fuck himself, I felt the stirrings of arousal. I'd purchased an instrument of humiliation as close to my penis as I could find. For a few moments, I'd actually wondered what his hole would feel like around my penis. I'd cupped my firming length behind the front of my slacks and was shocked that I'd felt something other than disinterest.

After my usual routine of making several wrong turns and the drive through the countryside, I pulled into my garage and leisurely made my way inside.

I finished the preparations I'd begun that morning. The metal plate under the end of my bed held the hook that I'd welded into place. At the end of the chain rested a shackle for Harrison's ankle. I'd provided him with a thick futon mattress on the floor at the foot of my bed. The chain was only long enough for him to reach the bathroom.

I walked to my dresser, changed my clothes and slipped the mask over my face. Then I placed the lifters in my shoes to add a few inches to my height. The leather of my gloves stretched and caressed over my hands. Whether it was Harrison's fear or the fact I hadn't allowed him near me in the years he worked for me—he hadn't worked out my identity. I had altered the tone of my voice when speaking with him while he's been my guest and I used my normal voice. Low and guttural, spoken sparingly. In my disguise that I used as a lawyer and normal human, I changed myself to fit —to blend with the more acceptable members of humanity.

On my way down to the basement, I retrieved the box I'd picked up for his items and the single bulb. I unlocked the bolts on the door and changed my steps to a heavier tread as I descended the stairs. My unhurried stride carried me to the center of the dark space to screw in the bulb. Then I approached his enclosure. He was lying on his side and tears were dried on his cheeks, his lashes matted. He shivered as he'd left the blanket off his body, but it was hugged to his chest.

I neared and crouched down, setting the box down and placed my hand over his side. Without touching him, I traced the curves of his body, and I wondered what his body hair would feel like under the planes of my hands. I leaned slightly to the side to find just the head of the dildo still inside his hole. His rim was swollen and red from the abuse. I slowly grabbed the base and shallowly fucked him with it. He was sufficiently stretched that it moved in and out of his hole smoothly. He whimpered in his sleep, but his exhaustion was clear as he didn't awaken. I knelt in the dirt and used my right hand to tug his cheeks apart to get a better view as I pushed the entire length into his hole.

I stopped as his back arched and then I roughly removed it. He yelped and put as much distance between us as possible. "Gather your things, place them in the box." I surged upward and backed up until I was just outside the opening.

"W-why?"

"Gather your things, place them in the box."

Tears once more filled his eyes, and an odd sense of excitement tightened my chest. His hands were shaking as he set each item in the box including the snacks he'd squirreled away under the mattress. The lantern and books were the last things to be tucked into the box.

"Stand and precede me upstairs, do not attempt to run... it will just make your punishment worse. Also, take your toy...you will wash it when we're upstairs."

He was barely able to get to his feet because he was trembling so violently. I knew what he was thinking, that he'd outlived his usefulness and I felt a sense of exhilaration at his fear. His steps stuttered, and he tripped as he froze at the bottom of the stairs. I pulled the chain to kill the light, and as soon as darkness took over the space, he moved upstairs.

His feet were caked in dirt, and he had smudges all over his body.

"Set your box aside and sit on the stool."

He obeyed so beautifully, and it caused an alien moment of feeling. I was unsure of what it was and pushed it aside for later analysis. I served him food and wine, all of which he consumed as a man savoring his last meal, and when I gave him a slice of cheesecake, the tears he'd restrained finally fell over his thick bottom lashes. That's when I realized his lashes were so thick and dark that they looked as if his eyes were lined with makeup. His beard that had started to turn shaggy didn't take away from how pretty I thought he looked.

I'd found people aesthetically pleasing. I recognized the superficial trappings of a person as beautiful or ugly, but I'd never felt pleasure in observing people. Except it wasn't any random person but Harrison.

"You will wash your dishes and your toy."

As he carried out his tasks, I drank a glass of water, and when I was satisfied, I ordered him to pick up his box and gave him directions upstairs to my bedroom. I didn't spend much time in my cabin and was impatient to return to my apartment, but until he'd accepted his place, we'd have to carry out his training here.

Over the next hour, I tended him without speaking. I bathed him, playing close attention to his genitals and his sore hole. He shied away but made no protests. I found it strangely satisfying to care for him. I even provided him with silk sleep pants that I dressed him in, and his suspicion grew the longer I didn't cause him pain. It was there in the way he stared at me.

I secured the shackle around his ankle, tucked him in bed and left him without a word to return downstairs to take care of my evening tasks, then clean myself up in the guest bath. Tonight, I'd let him believe whatever is going on in his head, but tomorrow I would begin the process of showing my ownership.

The act of forming attachments to things, people or places were as foreign to me as emotion. I was in territory I was unfamiliar with, and my own adjustments would take time. It was odd not to feel...homicidal.

Chapter Twelve

HARRISON

Before I'd opened my eyes that morning, I'd almost forgotten being held captive wasn't a nightmare. The bed was soft and the covers warm, the sleep pants comfortable on my skin. That had all dissolved at the intrusion of reality at the weight of the shackle and my view of an open bedroom door and feet of highly polished wood floors between me and escape. I'd found that the chain was long enough for me to reach the toilet and sink, but not the windows with the sheer curtains. What I could see of the view outside was acres of treetops.

It didn't give me any indication if I was still near home or not. I sat on my mattress, and the soreness of my hole further reminded me it wasn't a dream. My cheeks heated as I remembered the way he'd awakened me last night. I'd fallen asleep after an overwhelming sense of exhaustion had taken over me, and I'd cried until I had a headache. Before I realized it was my captor using the toy on me, I'd enjoyed a few moments of pleasure of being filled.

In the seconds after I awakened, I'd studied his face. Yes, he wore a mask, but the line of his unsmiling mouth didn't change. His eyes were still emotionless inside the holes of leather. The thinness of his frame made me wonder if he was naturally slim or did he not eat regularly. His clothes were always clean, wrinkle and debris free. I tried to assess if he was deranged and impulsive, but he rarely seemed to lose his calm even during the numerous punishments.

Afterward, when he'd ordered me to pack up the things he'd given me, or I'd collected, I knew he was going to kill me. He'd given me a full meal, the wine hit me harder than it should've, but I didn't normally drink alcohol. I ate each bite slowly as I was trying to prolong my death that I was sure was coming.

Although, that's not what happened. He'd bathed me, and he was gentle as he'd used a sponge with a soap that had a clean scent. I kept opening my mouth to demand that he get it over with, but I'd bitten my tongue until it hurt. The moment he'd tucked me into bed and drew the covers over me, I'd started to relax my guard.

He was being too...nice. I got up to use the bathroom and drink from the sink, then returned to my bed. It was the first time he'd left the house since I'd arrived without leaving provisions for the day. Part of me hoped that meant he wouldn't be gone long and another side told me I could stand to lose a few pounds. His punishment had to make up for the tenderness he showed.

No matter how much sleep I got while I was alone, the emotional and mental repercussions were taking their toll on me. I felt my fear should be greater, but I'd resigned myself to the fact that my captor could kill me at any time. It was the uncertainty of when it would happen that I couldn't take.

The closing of a door caused me to curl back up under

the covers to pretend I was asleep. I didn't know how much it would help, but I had to try to see if he would ignore me. I listened so I could follow his movements. He didn't seem in a hurry to come to the bedroom. From what I remembered of the first floor, he was in the kitchen. The sound of pans banging carried on for a few moments and then it was all eerily silent.

I was about to relax until I heard his heavy steps on the stairs. He always seemed to warn me when he was coming, and it amped up my anxiety. I was sure that's why he did it. It was the anticipation of pain and now humiliation.

"Your respirations are too high to be sleeping."

I almost did a double-take at the odd dry humor as if I was stupid for trying to avoid him. I had a feeling the man didn't have a clue as to how to be human.

"Stand up. Place your hands on the wall and wait."

I peeked at him to find a thick, black paddle in his hand and he tapped it against his left leg. I struggled to my feet as I was already anticipating the pain. Unlike the whip or his hand, the paddle was an unforgiving surface. I almost wished he would just spank or whip me, yet that didn't seem like his plan. He motioned to the empty wall between the bedroom and bathroom doors. There was no chance of escape if I ran. The padlock secured my tether to a steel plate. I'd studied it a few minutes before I'd fallen asleep last night.

Approaching the wall, I raised my hands to place them on the flat, cool surface and felt the subtly of brush strokes. I wanted something other than the punishment for an unknown offense to focus on. If I just braced and took it, the sooner the torment would end. My sleep pants were pulled over my ass with such force the waistband cut into my skin.

"I'm sure you've noticed your new situation."

"Y-yes, sir."

"New rules are in place. You will repeat each rule. The paddle will teach you what to expect if you break my rules."

I swallowed hard. "Yes, sir."

"Good boy. Let us begin by repeating your previous rules. Rule one...you will follow each order as given."

The first strike of the smooth surface forced me onto my toes. "I will follow each order."

"Rule two...you will thank me for each lash, paddling, and spanking given."

The second was harder than the first. I screamed. "Thank you for each...lash"—a leather-covered hand squeezed my right cheek—"paddling and spanking given."

My body twisted and I pressed my hot cheek against the cool wall. "Rule three...you will be ready to please me."

"I will please you, sir." Instead of squeezing my cheek as he'd done before, he slid his fingers into my crease and teased over my already sore hole. Then his chest was to my back, and his cock was a firm ridge. Usually, he wasn't hard when he pressed against me. As quick as he was there, his overwhelming presence behind me disappeared, and I didn't like where my thoughts were headed. If he was hard, didn't that mean he was going to use me in other ways to amuse himself? But he didn't disgustingly rut on my ass or paw at my crotch.

He confused me with the quickness of his mood changes. One minute his voice soft and caring, then next hard and unforgiving. I didn't prepare for the next hit and heat bloomed viciously as the pain radiated throughout my body.

"Rule four...you will not attempt to escape. I will kill you."

"I will not escape or you will...kill me."

Each rule seemed to intensify the strength of his strikes. I was told not to pleasure myself without his permission. I would prepare meals and clean, a small sliver of hope infused my agony at the thought that taking care of the house meant I wouldn't be chained.

My ass was on fire and the skin tight from the abuse. I whimpered as he grazed over the ravaged curves with the hard edge of the paddle. The touch barely there, but the paddling had inflamed the nerves, and it almost felt like another hit. My vision was blurry from tears, and my jaw ached from clenching my teeth. I sagged in relief as I noticed from the corner of my eye that he leaned the offending weapon on the wall. My reprieve didn't last long as his long, slender hands came to rest on my hips and curved around to the thick nest of my pubes.

Then his left hand was gone, and when it returned, so did my fear. After days or weeks of my cock in the cage, he removed it, the metal clanking to the floor between my feet. Suddenly he stroked my flaccid cock, and his other hand was shoved between our bodies. I heard no change in his breathing or any sound come from him as he finger-fucked me and jacked my cock. Shame came over me as my dick started to harden. He was pressed fully to my bruised ass sending mixed signals of pain and pleasure.

"So good."

My chaotic thoughts couldn't tell if he was saying I was good or if he was implying something else. Instead of pain taking me to my tiptoes this time, it was ecstasy. I fought it with everything in me, but no one other than myself had ever gotten me off. He'd hurt me, but now he seemed to want something else. If I gave in, what did that say about me? His thrusts and strokes grew in speed and roughness, and then my body betrayed me. I slammed my ass back against him and came with a shout, and he kept working me until I whimpered.

I was left adrift when he was just gone. I turned to find him observing me as if he were trying to work out an experiment. From the tenting at the front of his pants, he wasn't completely unaffected, but nothing in his expression gave it away. He must have caught me staring at his crotch because without preamble he undid the belt, button, and zipper. I realized that the dildo he'd made me fuck myself with was an inch shorter and notably slimmer than the cock he exposed. The black hair at the base of his cock was sparse, and his balls were bare.

I turned away as he started to stroke himself.

"On your knees, clean up your mess with your tongue. Wall and floor."

I clenched my fists as I knelt and tears once more filled my eyes as I licked my release where it splattered on the wall and the drops on the floor. As soon as I was done, all I heard were his steps retreating and leaving me alone. I struggled to my feet as everything hit me at once. My captor, the man who punished me for breaking his rules, had gotten me off, and my body had let it happen. For a second in my weakness, I had forgotten that I was a thing to him. So starved for touch that I'd allowed the man to paddle me, to fuck me and then he humiliated me further by making me clean my own cum up with my mouth.

With all the strength I had left, through tears and sobs, I washed myself, then returned to my mattress. I didn't feel like myself, I was confused and lost, and I didn't understand what was wrong with me. If I ever made it out of here, nothing would be the same, because my captor had broken something and I didn't know how to fix it.

Chapter Thirteen

COWEN

When I'd returned home from the office after allowing law enforcement to go through Harrison's computer, I'd reached my limit of interacting with people. I'd started a casserole for lunch. I'd searched recipes online in order to find something quick to make. Once I'd done that, I'd put my mask on and headed up to my bedroom. Harrison had pretended to sleep and badly, the pace of his breathing had given him away. Last night I had allowed him to settle into his new room. I'd treated him kindly and even dressed him.

Today was about learning his new role in our home. He'd taken the paddle beautifully. His screams and whimpers were perfect. When my penis had hardened, I'd waited for it to deflate as soon as his punishment ceased. I'd even prolonged his training so that I could enjoy the strangeness of the situation. To my shock, my length hadn't softened, and the ache was pleasurable.

I hadn't planned to reward him, but I wanted to test his tightness around my fingers, and I found jacking his cock enjoyable. My intent wasn't to gift him pleasure, that didn't give me the experience I required. Pain and humiliation were so much more complex sensations. Pleasure was fleeting—a momentary respite. For an unwanted moment, I had imagined replacing my fingers with my length. Coming was such a vulgar act, sharing bodily fluids with someone else. There was sweat and seed.

While I'd attempted sex before, I stopped when I didn't find anything appealing about the process. He tempted me, and when I'd exposed myself, he'd turned away. Something had flared hot in my chest, and I forced him to clean up his mess. I'd left him alone for hours allowing him time to think, but it was time for lunch. First, he was going to give me something.

I made my way upstairs to find him curled on his side beneath his blanket. The tie on my dresser caught my attention, and I grabbed it, then approached him. I leaned forward and ripped the cover from him, and he jerked away, pressing his back to the footboard of my bed. Without giving him a warning, I looped the tie around his throat. I wrapped the silk in my fist until it was tight around his neck, a turn of my wrist would tighten it further to control him.

He stared up at me with wide, frightened eyes, and when I started to undo my pants, I saw the second realization filled his gaze. I fisted my hand around the base of my cock and removed it from my pants. It was flushed with blood, the veins stood out starkly and fluid beaded at the slit. I painted his lips with precum. His breath was a warm caress across the damp head.

"Suck me," I ordered, and I waited out the indecision I observed on his face.

"I've never—"

"You only need to know how to take mine."

He opened his mouth, his tongue peeked out, and at the first lick, my length jerked. I barely kept in a groan.

"Open your mouth and stick out your tongue."

He did as I ordered, and I placed my fat head on his tongue, tapping it then pushing forward to give him a few inches. I paused taking in the wetness and heat, the texture of his tongue and palette, the softness of his lips and the coarseness of his beard. I pulled the tie until his mouth opened wider on a gasp and gave him more. While I debated whether to fuck his face and teach him a lesson or draw it out to analyze the newness, I slid slowly over his tongue.

I didn't know how to react. I was feeling, and it was too foreign. I released my dick and tied the strip of fabric around one of the slats of the footboard until I knew he wouldn't be able to move. Stepping forward, I planted my feet on either side of his legs and took his head in my hands. The strands of his hair felt like raw silk against my wrists. His lips were stretched tight around my girth. As I started a slow thrust and retreat, I never took my attention from his expression. I cataloged every gag, the saliva that ran from the corners of his mouth and his grunts when the head tapped the back of his throat.

Occasionally I would pull him forward until the tie tightened and restricted his breathing, I didn't relent until he frantically tapped my thigh. The slender muscles in my thighs contracted until they shook and I continued to fuck his face. I waited for the graze of teeth or him taking advantage, because like this, he was more in control than I was. He had every opportunity to hurt me. I dropped my head back as I increased my pace, restricted his breathing, and repeated until the nasty, wet sounds of my cock fucking his throat became all I could hear.

I'd never felt anything like it, and I barely kept myself under control until I felt and heard his first moan. I jerked my head up to stare down at him and found his eyes closed, and he sucked loudly as I tried to pull out. The strength drawing me back in and I noticed he even choked himself to get at my cock. He was drooling, grunting and gagging, it turned louder and messier every time he tightened the tie around his own throat.

"Is that what my boy wants?"

I didn't recognize my own voice since it was deeper and harsher. I curled my hands around his throat, pressed my thumbs tight to either side of Harrison's windpipe until his breathing was only a rasp from his throat.

"Such a good little slut. You want sir's cum. So greedy for it."

I released his throat, and he choked as he tried to breathe in around my cock, then he drew ragged breaths through his nose. My sac drew up tight, and I was done playing with my boy, I held his head in place and fucked his mouth until I thrust forward all the way. His beard tickled my nuts, and his nose was buried in the hair at my groin. I came so hard my body curled forward, and my frame jerked with each pulse. I shallowly ground against his mouth and didn't stop until the pleasure ebbed.

"Grab the footboard, now," I ordered as I pulled out and dropped to my knees.

I ripped the front of his pants down until the fabric was tucked under his hairy balls. When I laid my forehead to his, I started to jack his cock that looked red and angry making him whimper, and I loathed the leather of my gloves that kept me from feeling his skin. Without thought, I moved in close enough to wrap both our dicks in my hand. The skin along his length was hot and soft. It only took him a few strokes, and his release covered my hand and head of my cock. I suddenly realized I found his scent pleasant. His body was twice as broad as mine. His own length was shorter and slenderer than mine. His body was covered in hair and I...liked it in comparison to my hairless one.

My head was too full of information and details. Too many scents. I untied him and lifted my hand to his mouth.

"Clean up your mess, boy."

He seemed in a trance or as if he'd come out of deep sleep. He didn't rush the cleaning of my glove, as he sucked two fingers into his mouth, I remembered what it felt like around my penis.

I needed to think. I unlocked Harrison's shackle, helped him to his feet and took him to the bathroom to clean up. Fifteen minutes later, I had him seated at the island in my kitchen and served him food and drink. He had yet to say a word, and I didn't complain. I required quiet to work through the new developments.

He ate his food slowly as I drank a glass of water. He refused to look at me, and I wondered if he were as confused as I was. He was supposed to take my punishment. Take care of my home, and when he had agreed that he was mine, I would return him to civilization but not until he pledged himself to me. He was greedy, silently begging me for everything I gave him.

Keeping him was only supposed to be temporary, and in a matter of days, something had changed. I needed to figure out what it was because I didn't like loose ends. Everything needed to be in its place. My routine was key to existing. He had perplexed me, and I didn't like it. It didn't fit.

Harrison, my assistant, was shy, silent and frightened of me. But my captive was greedy, and he was beginning to find pleasure in the pain. Was he leading me into a false sense of security or did he want to remain as mine—my thing to care for and use for pleasure I wasn't supposed to feel.

I turned away to refill my glass, and I felt his gaze on me in the sensation of the hairs lifting on the back of my neck. Did he plot even now to escape? He would be mistaken if he thought I'd ever free him. He was mine, and I would prove it in pain and pleasure, I owned him. Would always own him. If pain was what he needed, I was the one to give it to him.

I still felt the thrust of his cock, the slight soreness from his strong hands and the tie around my throat. My dick hardened at the forbidden thrill of him controlling even the breaths I took. He was gentle afterward, jacked my cock until I came for him and then bathed me, and fed me. I was more confused than ever. This was the first day I was left on my own.

For hours after he left, I'd stayed on my mattress waiting for the setup. Was he lurking quietly downstairs to punish me? What if I tried to escape? It had taken two hours of pep talk before I'd headed to the kitchen. The list of chores tacked to the front of the fridge with a plain steel colored magnet caught my attention. The block letters were perfectly aligned, so they possessed no clue to his identity. It didn't show personality—no flourishes.

The items were normal things that I did at home every day except for the last item, but I didn't want to think about that. I'd made my way through the list quickly. As I cleaned, I didn't spot any pictures. The cabin interior looked like staged sets for a design magazine shoot. It was a cold, sterile environment, very much like the man. Along with an absence of personal touches, he didn't have a television or even a radio. The laptop in his office was password protected.

I liked noise. I'd even taken extra care with the vacuuming just to listen to the whirr. I felt stupid cleaning a spotless house. My captor screamed OCD. While I was afraid of him, I was also disturbed by my fascination with him. For most of my life I'd taken care of my mother, and while I loved her, it was freeing to not be in charge. I didn't have to worry because he provided everything I needed.

Although, wasn't that a part of Stockholm Syndrome? Our will broken to adapt to life as a captive, but I almost felt content. I broke the rules, and I was punished. I did something right, and I earned a reward. No one liked punishment, but weren't we under the will of laws in the real world?

I didn't have anything else to clean, so I put away the vacuum and cleaning supplies. My list of duties said to have dinner ready at six. I'd checked out the kitchen that morning. It was fully stocked. I loved to cook, but it always seemed a waste to do it for one. I lived on takeout and snacks.

I closed the hallway closet and turned toward the front door. I'd stood there earlier, on the precipice of escaping. For a few seconds, I had the door open. The scent of trees, a cool breeze, and I could've easily run. If he was in the city, I could be far away by the time he made it back to the cabin. Instead, I closed it and went back to the tasks. He wouldn't keep me forever. Soon he'd grow tired of me and maybe want to move someone else into the cellar.

Part of me hoped that he wanted to keep me—how sick did that make me? I'd started to believe that even within the punishments and humiliation that he cared. He kept me on edge. One minute he hurt me and the next he was gentle. It was as if he were conditioning me for something, but I just didn't know what.

As I kept a close eye on the time, I began to prepare dinner. When he fed me, I hadn't once seen him eat. He was slim but strong, and a little over six foot tall. My curiosity grew at what the mask concealed. I studied the voice and tried to remember if I'd heard it before. He always concealed himself in every way. He'd yet to touch me without gloves. My captor seemed to keep a physical and emotional distance.

I wanted the mask gone but also didn't—once he removed it, I'd know his face and didn't that mean there was the potential to identify him. Uncertainty and fear caused me to shake as I checked that last item on the chore list.

Be naked and waiting when I arrive home.

As soon as the clocks little hand touched six, I heard the door open, and I hastily shoved my sleep pants down my legs. My full focus landed on the soft fabric I folded carefully. I'd made pasta and sauce, but I didn't have time to...I felt his gaze boring into me, and I didn't like his silence. I slowly lifted my gaze, taking in the expensive black suit paired with a charcoal dress shirt and black tie. I paused there waiting for some order—anything, but he just remained silent.

"I see you've done as I asked."

At the sound of the voice, I jerked my head up in surprise and looked right at Cowen.

"What..."

"I'm surprised you didn't figure it out by now. But I must admit my work voice differs from my real one."

The tone Cowen used at work was smoother and enunciated, while my captor's was low and almost growly. It was an odd contrast. Why hadn't I noticed? I'd studied the man while I was sure he wasn't looking. My embarrassment over my misplaced crush on him came back, and all the fantasies I had of Cowen set my cheeks on fire.

"Why?"

"Well, you did see me in the middle of my second job. And while I thought about killing you, keeping you held a bit of"—he paused—"fascination."

I backed up holding the sleep pants in front of my groin. Memories slammed into me. I'd caught sight of a man striking another and the sound of the victim's skull hitting concrete. "Is he dead?"

"Very much so. I was paid well for it."

"Why?"

Cowen looked confused at my question. His heavy dark brows were meeting as his forehead furrowed. "It was a job." His gaze drew down my body, and I hid behind the pants. I'd gotten used to my unknown captor keeping me naked, but I didn't like Cowen looking at me.

"Why did you do this to me?"

"Because I wanted to."

"I want to go home." Mortified at what I'd done—what I'd allowed him to do—all I could think about was getting away from him. I didn't even care if he killed me.

The silence became oppressive as I backed farther away, tucked myself into a corner. My gaze didn't leave the floor, even though I didn't hear one step, the toes of Cowen's dress shoes appeared. Once he was right there, I noticed he was shorter than my captor and seemed slimmer. "You're different."

"Lifts in my shoes and padding here and there. Do you like your captor better?"

I rolled my lips between my teeth and refused to answer. A choked yell turned to a groan as it left my compressed throat when Cowen squeezed cutting off my oxygen. It wasn't like when I'd given him a blowjob. My hands came up to claw at his hand and wrist, the pressure built in my face and my chest ached as I struggled to take in even a small breath. Just as my eyes started to roll and I felt my vision fading, I wheezed as the fingers unexpectedly loosened and I fought to draw air into my lungs.

"You think you have power here? You do not. I could kill you without remorse just as I originally planned. You liked it when I was a stranger...you begged for my cock."

"You hate me."

"I should. Yet, I don't."

He released me quick enough that I stumbled and he put distance between us. He casually checked over what I'd made for dinner as if I wasn't losing my mind. My head hurt from memories and stress. I bent to grab my sleep pants.

"No. I requested you be naked."

I straightened and cupped my hands over my crotch. It was stupid. Cowen knew every inch of me. I was hiding a body he'd studied countless times over the weeks I'd been there. The calendar on his desk had told me I'd been there nearly a month, and I didn't feel as if so many days had passed.

"I purchased you a present, but you've failed to earn it with your actions. It may be appropriate to move you back to the basement." His voice was cold and gave nothing away.

The disappointment at his words sickened me, and I almost started crying at his disapproval. "Why...why are you keeping me?"

"I own you."

"Why?"

Earlier I'd felt I was settling into what I'd come to think of my new life. Again, I felt as if something was broken inside me. That I'd allowed Cowen—a stranger—to use me as he saw fit and I submitted.

"I don't know. I was quite happy with my celibate life. Sex is a vulgar and disgusting act, but I enjoy playing with you. You look pretty sucking my cock."

He stated it with the same emotion someone would relay the weather for the day.

"Don't you feel anything?"

"Emotion is a waste of energy."

"Then why keep me if you're—"

"Once you pledged yourself to me, you were to be allowed to return to work, but I see that we've lost ground. Therefore, gather your things so that I may return you to the basement."

A sob caught in my throat because I didn't want to be put back in the darkness. "I don't want to go back down there."

"Then you earned punishment. Return to our room and place the shackle around your ankle. You will wait for me on your knees."

Neither of my options made me feel safe, pain or darkness, both I hated. I dropped my chin to my chest and did as he ordered. Just as I passed him, he fisted his hand in my hair, winching my head back. His slim body pushed flush to my back, and his breath was hot behind my ear. I existed in this limbo between pleasure and pain, the burn of my scalp, but I hated when he punished me. How did he reduce me to whimpering with nothing more than jerking my head back—using me?

"You can deny, but you love it when I use you. You love

someone else in charge—guiding and punishing you when you make mistakes. You may lie to yourself, but for three years, I listened to those submissive *yes, sirs* that fell from those pretty lips. You wanted me to hurt you."

"I don't—" I cried out when his grip twisted my head until his lips almost touched mine. His gaze was cold and vacant. I nearly came when he grabbed my dick in a tight hold.

"You do. You crave the lash of my whip. The sting of my hand. You beg with every look for me to fuck that pretty mouth. You love that I hold your life in my hands. Lie to me again."

The monstrous cock that didn't fit his skinny frame pushed at my bare ass. His slacks were the only protection between us. Unlike my time in the basement where his body showed no response, he was hard. My brain urged me to fight—to run—my body had other plans.

"Kiss me, sir."

"That would be a reward, of which you are undeserving."

The words forming in my mind frightened me, but I parted my lips and let them free. "Punish me then." I couldn't lie any longer, and I hated myself for these new and frightening cravings. I didn't like being in charge—agonizing over every decision, worrying if it was right or wrong. He took that burden from me and as sick as that made me, I was too weak to give it up. I wanted him to keep me. I'd longed for Cowen since I interviewed for the job as his office manager. I'd enjoyed his control in the office, and now that I knew he was my captor, I wanted more.

I'd fought it so hard, and I was tired. I gasped as he pushed me away, and as I turned to him, he handed me a paper bag.

"Take it upstairs, use the items to ready yourself for me. I will come for you when I'm done working. When I come upstairs, you will be on the bed with your plug in and ready to take my cock. Am I understood?"

"Yes, sir."

"Go." He turned away as he dismissed me.

I wanted to question, to ask what was in the bag, but I slowly strode through the house and upstairs to the bedroom. When I entered the bathroom, I opened the bag to find several boxes, my face flamed at the items inside. I was embarrassed as I read the directions and knelt on the floor, bending forward. For the next hour, I prepared myself, taking a long shower and savoring the hot water. I used lubed fingers to prepare my ass for the massive plug. As much as I wanted to linger, I needed to be ready when he came for me.

I ran the smooth lengths of ropes through my hands as I unhurriedly took the stairs to the second floor. Once I'd dismissed him, I'd cleaned up the minimal mess in my kitchen and stored the food for later. I'd stayed in my office working until I heard the water stop and gave him a few minutes to comply with my order to be waiting in the bed. All day I'd imagined what I had planned for him. I'd decided to reveal who I was only for the fact I wanted to keep him. It still confused me—the possessiveness that I had for Harrison. I'd spent my life alone, hating everyone and everything, killing without remorse for work and fun.

I'd excelled at many things over my lifetime, but killing was the one I took the most pride. Although I'd felt content with my existence, something inside me had shifted when I'd met Harrison. It was all disorienting wanting someone. When I'd entered the kitchen, I enjoyed the sight of him standing in my home naked and waiting for me. I felt something I assumed was disappointment when he found me lacking and his faceless captor worth more.

When I made it to my room, I let my gaze move over

him where he lay stiffly on my bed. I approached silently and draped the ropes over the footboard, grabbing one. I placed my knees on the mattress and knelt beside him, I secured one end of the rope around his ankle, looping it around his knee. I fed it through the slats of the headboard, pulling until I drew his leg to the side exposing him for me. I repeated on the other limb until I could see the large base of the plug I'd bought for him. His legs were pulled back enough that his ass was tipped off the mattress.

"Do you know what I'm going to do to you?" As I slipped off the bed, I asked unconcerned with his answer. I strode to my closet and removed my shoes. Until he had asked me to let him go, I'd enjoyed the newness of my erection, but now I was angry that my body responded to him. I darted a glance over my shoulder. "Well?"

"No."

"I'm going to fuck you." I stripped and placed each item in the dry-cleaning bag until I stood naked. My scars and ugliness on display. I turned to face the bed and heard him gasp. *Was it shock or disgust?*

"What happened to you?"

"Reminders of the mistakes I've made and why they're never repeated. Did you do as I asked?"

His face turned red, and his only answer was a nod.

I closed the distance between us, stopped briefly for the lube in the nightstand drawer. I crawled onto the bed and sat on my heels when I positioned myself between his legs. I took the base of the plug in my left hand and tugged until his reddened hole stretched around it. He whimpered, and I let it go to watch it sink back into his ass. While I continued to pull at the plug, I surged forward to wrap my hand around his throat, squeezing until he started to claw again at my wrist like he'd done earlier in the kitchen.

My cock jerked as I eased my hold and he drew in a ragged breath. I did it again and again, each time fucking him harder with the plug until the silicone slapped against his skin. Instead of fighting me, he tapped my wrist when he needed a breath. I wasn't gentle as I removed the plug and set it aside.

"Do you think you've earned my cock, boy?" I had to stop touching him in order to slick my length, and it was painful. Sensations I'd never dreamed existed overwhelmed me with their intensity. My mind was flooded with all the possibilities that my body's response could conjure.

"N-no," he answered. But even as he did, Harrison rolled his hips as his body trembled from head to toe.

His heavy body was already covered in sweat that glistened in his body hair.

"So you think you deserve punishment?"

"I—I don't know, sir."

He squealed as I spanked the lower curves of his cheeks where they met his thighs, then repeating the strikes until the skin rose with the welts of my hands. I felt my breathing pick up so fast that my chest hurt. My concave stomach pulled in tighter, making my ribs stand out more starkly. I placed my thumb under his heavy balls and circled my fingers around his cock, constricting until he whimpered. His cock and balls turned red. I slicked my cock and placed it at his hole. I thrust and pushed his body up the bed—the heat and tightness shocked me.

I measured my cock in his hole, once, twice and a third time. The rim squeezed the base of my dick like a cockring. I memorized the sensation, analyzed the emotions I felt and realized sweat was trickling down my temples. My gaze moved to his face, and he watched me with teary eyes. I frowned at that expression. I released his cock and blanketed his body with mine. The hair on his chest and stomach tickled my skin.

I drew my hips backward and slammed forward, and his deep grunt fanned his breath across my mouth. He asked for a kiss earlier. I don't know what came over me, but I brushed my lips to his. I felt awkward as I kissed him. Blindly, I reached out and tugged the ends of the ropes freeing his legs.

The urge to hurt him faded away as he returned my kiss. He didn't fight or attempt to pull away. His heels dug into my ass cheeks. It was all too overwhelming, the pleasure too much. He parted his lips, and his tongue touched mine—I jerked away. His face was flushed and the waves of his hair stuck to his forehead and temples.

"I've never done this before."

He confessed his inexperience before he'd sucked my cock. I didn't understand the covetousness over the fact that he'd known no other cock but mine. I frantically searched for another point of reference in my life where I'd felt this and I couldn't find a single second to compare.

He touched me. His fingertips stroked along my sides and down to my hips. I enjoyed his softness and the way it conformed to my thin frame. I pulled away completely, and then the tears did start—they wet his cheeks, and my cock got harder.

"On your hands and knees." He obeyed so sweetly for me, and soon his hairy ass was in the air, his face buried in the pillows. I added more slick to my dick and came up behind him. Then I placed the fat head at his hole. I rammed into him without warning. His back arched and his head tipped backward. I gripped his hips and fucked him.

"Tell me, boy, who owns you?"

"You do."

I rode him and realized that he pushed back just as hard as I thrust. His ass bounced, and I froze. "Take it, boy."

He started slowly, pushing backward, rolling his hips as he worked his ass on and off my dick. He screamed and begged like a pretty little slut. He clenched every time he rocked forward.

I was done letting him play. I wanted the orgasm I felt building—my first where I'd fill his ass with cum. I leaned over his back, fisted my hand in his hair and wrapped the free one around his throat. As soon as I controlled his breathing, his movements went wild, and I fucked him with every ounce of my strength. I eased my grip every few seconds, let him catch his breath only to choke him again. His entire body stiffened, and he whimpered in his throat, and I released his hair. Shoving my hand under him to find his cock slicked with cum.

I straightened, retook his hips, and I dropped my gaze to his hole, watching as my length disappeared. His ass was red from the abuse, and I pounded into his limp body.

"Beg me for my cum."

I pulled out until nothing but the head was inside him, and he grabbed my hips, his nails painfully dug into my flesh.

"Beg."

"Give me your cum, sir."

"You want me to fill you? Let you feel it leak out later?"

"Yes, sir."

"Tell me you're my slut."

"I'm your slut, sir. Give it to me, sir."

With piston-hard snaps of my hips, I gave him my cock over and over, my release refusing to come. Every muscle in my body pulled tight to the point of pain, but still, I couldn't get off. Frustration turned to anger, so I used him harder and rougher. I felt it was right there, but I couldn't get there.

I jerked from him, angry at him and my body. He turned over and stared at me. His cock was again semi-hard. I took him again. I slammed my mouth violently onto his, and he clawed at my back. I felt the skin split beneath the pressure of nails he hadn't cut in weeks. I lowered my face to his neck and bit, causing him to throw his head back. I left marks over his throat, shoulders, and chest as I pounded him.

"Sir, it hurts, cum in my ass, please."

My balls drew up, and my body pulled into an arch as I released, slick and cum making wet sex sounds as I fed his ass my cock. I was forcing him to take every drop. Cum dribbled from his ass wetting my balls and his ass. I didn't stop until it was agony to move and I left him. I grabbed his hard, red cock and jacked him as he writhed on the bed, screaming and calling my name, not sir, but Cowen in a desperate litany. Cum splashed onto my stomach and covered my hand as he relaxed into a sweaty, exhausted heap on the bed.

"Clean up your mess, boy."

He struggled to sit up and then moved until he was on his hands and knees to lick his cum from my stomach. I combed my fingers through his hair. His tongue was hot and wet where it moved over my stomach and pelvic bones.

"Good boy. You're sir's prefect little slut."

While he cleaned my stomach, I picked up the plug and reinserted it. He shoved his face into my stomach. "You keep it in. I'm not done using that ass. When I'm done, you'll feel empty without me every second of your days and nights. Do you understand, boy?"

"Yes, sir."

"Are you mine?"

"Yes, sir."

"Will you always stay with me?"

"Yes, sir."

His gaze came up to mine, and I saw the honesty in his eyes. Saw the promise there. A sense of contentment came over me, that's all I could assume it was as I'd never experienced it before. He was mine, and I wasn't letting him go. I'd always wanted to understand what others felt, and he would always give me that. I should've realized it before, but I'd come so close to losing it and Harrison.

Chapter Sixteen

HARRISON

I groaned as I slowly awakened and snuggled under the covers. The bed was super comfortable, and I was so warm. I started to nuzzle into my pillow, and the feeling of a lean, smooth chest against my cheek had me slowly opening my eyes. Then the night before came back to me with the impact of a sledgehammer. He'd removed the ropes then had taken me to the bathroom to shower with him.

The tenderness that he'd shown was almost dizzying. One minute he was brutal and punishing and the next he'd fucked me with such passion and need. He'd taken me three times over the night. The way he'd looked—his face flushed and his breathing harsh—I'd been amazed at the controlled Cowen losing his cool. He took the reins so easily—knew exactly what I craved and how much to give; he knew when to ease off.

Every muscle in my body ached, my hole was raw and still stretched with the plug. Each time he'd cum inside me, he'd replaced the toy. He seemed to want his sign of ownership to remain in my body.

His breathing was deep and even beneath my cheek. I didn't move as I let my gaze move over him. His body was covered in scars, and the ones on his arms couldn't be anything other than self-inflicted. He had patches of thick raised tissue that looked like burn marks. He was even missing hunks of flesh. I was concerned by the thinness of his frame. Although, I liked that he was smaller than me but able to dominate me so easily.

What I loved the most was that his response said he didn't find my body lacking. I'd grown content in the body I was blessed with, but I'd never found it appealing in other people's eyes.

I brought my fingers to my lips and remembered his kiss. It had been awkward as if he hadn't done it before or at the very least rarely. I didn't know what to think of the new development. I'd assumed when he ordered me upstairs that I'd earned a punishment for telling him I wanted to leave. His rage had clearly shown on his face and in his eyes. I didn't anticipate that he would be my first.

When he'd asked me was I his and would I stay, I hadn't hesitated to answer yes. When he was just my captor, I'd accepted that he would keep me until the moment he was tired of me. Now that I knew it was Cowen, I wanted to be his. I'd wanted him for years. I'd imagined Cowen loving on me in my dreams. Now, it was a reality, and I didn't want to go anywhere.

I didn't believe it was love. I wouldn't hold my feelings or his to such a lofty position. Did I believe he'd keep me forever? No, but even a limited time was better than none. I loved the way he filled me. The passion he showed when he pushed me over the precipice of desire I'd never felt in my life.

"Turn over on your side."

I gasped at the gruff order and obeyed, and the plug was eased from my raw hole. I whimpered as I was filled with every thick, hard inch.

"Mine, boy."

The words were nothing but a feral growl as he slammed his hips to my ass. The high-pitched grunt almost embarrassed me as he fucked me. He told me he owned me with every word and action. I drew my left leg to my chest to open myself further. His possession was everything I'd always needed and never knew I could have.

THREE WEEKS LATER

Two weeks after I'd promised to stay with him, he'd allowed me to come back to work, but unlike before, I went home with Cowen every night. Sometimes back to his cabin or the penthouse apartment he kept in the city.

My new reality still took some adjustment. I'd nearly had a panic attack when I'd had to deal with the detectives that had looked for me. Lying wasn't a skill I possessed, but Cowen had taken care of my story. I just needed time away —a vacation. In some ways, it was a twisted truth. I'd discovered something about myself while held captive by him. I liked being taken care of and not having to worry about things.

He made sure I ate, slept, he'd even helped me pack up my things and move to his place. I loved my mother and wouldn't regret the years I had with her, even the ones that I acted as her caretaker. When I'd walked back into my house, it had felt more like a prison than the basement had. The memories were too much.

I still wondered if something was wrong with me. How easily I'd accepted the relationship. I lived for the lash of his whip. He grounded me when I felt lost. He rewarded me when I did something right. Most of my days were spent working with a plug in and ready for when he needed me. He fucked me numerous times a day. I relished the ache after he used me. Yet, my favorite reward out of everything was his kisses.

The way he wanted me was unrestrained. He didn't hide it, and when his cock would harden, he'd call me. I had a feeling that he'd never kissed before. It made the act more special for me.

The nights he left, he didn't lie about where he was going. I wondered how many people he'd killed. As soon as I started to think about it, I pushed the thoughts away. It was a part of him he never brought into the house or apartment. Some part of me was still terrified of his silences and coldness, as if I knew that one day, he'd grow bored with me.

Today he was in court, and I was alone in the office. I didn't like it when he left me unaccompanied. My separation anxiety was at an all-time high.

The outer door opened and I pasted a smile on my face. A man in an expensive suit and a hundred-dollar haircut entered. The stranger was gorgeous in that distinguished way that made mere mortal men insecure. Elegant and handsome, rich and entitled, and he put me on edge.

"Good afternoon, how can I help you?"

"Is Mr. Kingsley in?"

We didn't get many walk-in clients, it was mostly by appointment, but I was always supposed to ask them to leave a message or schedule a time. Cowen didn't like being disturbed when he worked. Closed door meant not to bother him.

"No, sir, he's in court. Can I take a message or schedule a convenient time for a meeting?"

"No, I can wait."

I frowned as the guy unbuttoned his jacket and took a seat in one of a few chairs we had for clients.

"It could be a few hours."

"I have time. We have a bit of business to discuss." The man lazily crossed his legs and seemed to settle in for the wait.

"Okay." The man made me uncomfortable, and I'd let Cowen deal with the pushy man when he returned. "Would you like a cup of coffee or some water?"

"Coffee would be great, thank you."

"Milk and sugar?"

"Black is fine."

I went into the small room that acted as a breakroom and poured a cup of coffee. Something about the man was off, and I didn't know what to do except treat him like any other client. The man in the outer office wasn't any different than any other shady client Cowen had taken. Something about this one put me on edge, though.

I reentered the room and approached the stranger with a smile.

"Thank you, Harrison."

I backed up quickly as his fingers caressed over mine as he took the mug. The touch wasn't impersonal, neither was the heated gaze the man gave me.

"Cowen has...amazing taste in men."

I didn't like the way he drew his gaze down my body.

"Who are you?"

The man lazily drank his coffee with a small smile, but his eyes turned cold, darkening.

"Cowen has become lax in his job he does for me. I can't let his insubordination go unpunished. What kind of boss would that make me, Harrison?"

He made my name sound like a curse, as if it was my fault Cowen wasn't doing something for him. I hadn't once demanded anything from Cowen. Didn't fight him when he left to take care of jobs since I'd promise to stay with him.

I was about to answer when the door opened, and three men that made me look small entered with guns drawn.

"You're going to come with us. I had thought about just having a talk with Cowen, but really, this is a better option. I can take something which belongs to him."

Two of the men flanked me, and the other came up behind me. I was a big man, but I wasn't a fighter, and I was no match for the barrel of a gun digging painfully into my ribs. Cowen would come for me since I belonged to him, but maybe he would think it was too much trouble. Easier just to find another toy to play with when he was bored.

Cowen's employer set aside the mug and stood, then he did up the buttons of his jacket, smiling pleasantly at me like it was just a normal everyday conversation. Like they weren't using me for bait to lure Cowen out.

I was confused and terrified as I let them lead me from the office and down to a limo waiting at the curb. I started to get into the car, then fell inside between the seats as one of them pushed me. Quickly I rolled onto my back and stared up at them. Their calmness was scarier than Cowen's, and I'd seen the violence and cruelty he was capable.

"What are you going to do with me?"

"Harrison, we need to make an example. Cowen needs to learn there are repercussions for not doing as ordered. I pay him quite well for the service he provides."

The stranger talked as if Cowen didn't murder people for him. Cowen was quiet and intense, self-assured to the point of arrogance, but nothing made me overly anxious around him; not like the man smiling at me as if we were speaking about the weather.

"What does that have to do with me?"

"Well, it's quite simple, you're Cowen's weakness. I was shocked to discover that the cold-blooded bastard had a man. It's required that I know everything about my employees. Loved ones are the easiest weaknesses."

"Cowen won't come for me. He'll just replace me. You're wasting your time." It hurt because I believed the statement to be true. Sir may be possessive of me, but I had no illusions that he would go out of his way to rescue me. If he came, it would be to destroy the people who dared threaten him.

"I know quite a bit about Cowen. He committed his first murder before he reached puberty. A born killer and there has never been one as proficient as him. If you're going to be a hindrance in him working for me, then I must make an example of you. First, we'll send you to him piece by piece until he comes around to my way of thinking."

I'd survived the pain Cowen inflicted, but he didn't want to cause permanent damage. These men would whittle away at my body, and all they would earn was Cowen's rage. The arrogance of the man speaking to me would be his downfall. No one owned Cowen—never would.

Just as I'd accepted that my captor would kill me weeks ago, I did the same now. I would die, and there was nothing I could do about it. All I could hope for would be that they didn't draw it out. I'd have preferred them slitting my throat and leaving me for Cowen to find when he returned.

They would torture me as an example to a man who didn't work the way they thought. Cowen was more than a professional killer—assassin—as the man stated, Cowen was a born killer. He had the coldness and detachment from society which made him perfect for his job.

The double life Cowen lived required control and the ability to compartmentalize. Cowen looked...ordinary. Nothing about him was exceptional. When looking at Cowen, you'd never know what he was capable of doing. Seeing behind the mask had opened my eyes to the man my boss pretended to be and held no illusions. He wanted to fuck and own me, but I knew those days were numbered. This incident would just make it happen sooner.

It depressed me, but did I really have a place to complain?

"Cowen will come, but it won't be for me. He doesn't love me. He'll just kill you for the fun of it."

The man threw back his head as he let out a belly laugh.

"You poor boy. I don't care if he believes he loves you or not. I just want to destroy something he owns. You're only a means to an end."

"Then kill me."

"Not yet, I'm going to have some fun with you first."

He gripped my hair in a brutal grip, nothing like Cowen's and I turned my head, feeling the sharp burn to my scalp as I avoided him kissing me. They could do whatever they wanted to me, remove fingers or limbs, flay me alive, but they wouldn't use my body like that. That I would fight. Cowen was the only man who would ever love on me. I'd slit my own throat before I'd let this man or anyone else touch me.

Chapter Seventeen

COWEN

I'd found the note on my desk after I'd returned from court. For long minutes, I'd stared at the piece of paper and figured he'd gone back on his promise. It was something I'd expected, and I had no issues with fulfilling my promise to kill him. He knew too many of my secrets, yet when I read the letter that had all disappeared.

My employer apparently had an issue with me not taking every assignment issued to me. We'd always worked under the agreement that when I was done, it was over. The man was well aware of my reputation and what this would bring down on him. He hadn't left a time or place to meet.

I knew all their names. Their family and friends. I hadn't gone into this job without learning what I needed to survive. When I received his first inquiry, and we'd agreed never to make contact, that didn't mean I didn't have means to gather the intel for a hostile takeover.

If they'd tried to take me out, I wouldn't have held a grudge, but they took something that belonged to me. My boy had pledged himself to me. I sealed that promise by repeatedly filling him with my cum. Once I'd felt his ass around my cock, I'd lost all control. My body was insatiable. I didn't understand why it was only for him. I'd gone to a bar I'd visited in the past to check if he'd broken something inside me.

The men and women who'd occupied the bar, even the men who reminded me of him hadn't caused a response. I looked at them as marks—my next kill. I'd quickly left and returned to the cabin, only to find him naked and waiting on his knees beside our bed. I'd fucked his mouth until he drank every drop. The intensity of my awakening romanticisms was jarring, and I still didn't understand why it had all come to life only for him.

All I knew was that I didn't want to be without him. He'd accepted me. He made no fuss when I left him alone to take care of my assignments. He simply waited for me to come home. Each kill made me more desperate to fuck him —the momentary euphoria of the murder prolonged by my need to take him any way I wanted. He didn't argue or protest, just submitted.

I'd closed the office down and had put a note on the door saying we were closed due to a family emergency. I gathered supplies and mentally made a list of my targets. I'd start from the bottom and work my way up until I reached the top, Cristo. They were so much creatures of habit. They partied at the same bars. Fucked the same men and women, it was almost as if they'd grown lazy in their complacency. They believed themselves untouchable because Cristo supposedly owned the city.

I was the worst predator, more skilled than they knew. Killing sustained me, but there were worse things than death. I could've taken them down years ago. I had files on all of them that contained every dirty secret—where every body was buried.

~~~

I stood outside one of Cristo's clubs where his lower-level thugs partied. I'd changed my appearance with a wig and glued on a beard. My blade was tucked inside a sheath in my boot. I turned up the collar on my peacoat and made my way across the nearly deserted street. I was plain and drew only minimal attention. I entered the dark interior of the club.

My gaze scanned the scene, and the four I'd picked out were scattered around the room. I approached the bar and ordered a drink, then pretended to sip at it. One of my targets was tucked into a corner with a woman. I picked up my drink, and as I neared the table, I feigned drunkenness and dropped my drink beside them. I pulled the knife from my boot as I heard him bitching about men who couldn't handle their liquor. I struck, inserted the blade between his ribs, and he didn't even have time to call out for help.

Just as the woman came out of her shock, I blocked her from the room and drove the blade upward beneath her chin. I calmly posed them as if they were whispering to each other. I wiped the blade off on my black pants. *One down, three to go.* I wondered if one of them had touched my boy or even Cristo, maybe the bastard had left that job to his enforcers. Either way, tonight began the destruction of Cristo's organization.

I placed myself with a full view of the room and spotted the next one heading toward the bathroom. *Perfect,* I thought to myself as I weaved through the crowd and I blinked hard at the bright lights. The bastard stood at the urinal with his cheap suit ill-fitting on his bulky frame. I sidled up a few spots down from him, and I waited. He didn't pay any attention to me, and as he finished up, he turned to wash his hands.

My movements were graceful with years of practice as I shoved him into a stall. He fought, slamming my body back into the walls of the small enclosure. People had always taken my lack of size as a weakness. It had always turned out to be their greatest and last mistake. My arms tightened around his throat as I gripped his chin in my left hand. I jerked, hearing the crack of his neck snapping. I eased him onto the toilet. Pulling his pants down. After locking the door, I shimmied out from under the stall door.

The last two were easier. They were secretly fucking and always escaped out back for a quick fuck in the dark of the alley. I took the exit and slipped into the shadows. This one would be harder as my patience was quickly reaching its end. I knew what they were probably doing to my boy. They were smarter than I'd anticipated, they hadn't kept him in one of the many safehouses around the city where they conducted business or held bait until the person was useful.

My boy dying wasn't an option, but if they were stupid enough to touch what was mine, then I'd avenge him. Afterward, I'd move on to another city, maybe slip into retirement with a few freelance jobs to keep me occupied.

Minutes past, and as I was about to reenter the bar, the door opened and the men I was waiting for exited. They were locked in each other's arms. They kissed brutally as if fighting for dominance and I was disgusted by the display. There was a sweetness in earning submission. Harrison had given it to me, and I didn't have to fight him for it after he'd accepted that he was mine.

The bigger of the two men turned and offered his back, shoving his pants over his ass. The other came up behind him. Quickly grunts and curses filled the narrow alley. I waited until they were lost in lust and unaware of their surroundings. My soft-soled boots barely made a sound as I neared them. Even if I had walked normally, my steps would be lost in the sounds of their fucking.

I held the hilt firmly in my hand and thrust it forward, entering at the base of the big guy's skull and the other man yelled as the big guy fell to his knees. I cut off the man's next cry for help with an upward motion just as I'd done with the guy at the table. Piercing his back between his ribs to deflate his lung. Satisfaction filled me as I listened to the gurgling as the bastard drowned in his own blood.

The knife was carefully cleaned and returned to my boot. I left the alley as calm as if I was taking a midnight stroll. My heart rate hadn't even picked up pace. As I started to turn the corner at the end of the block, shouts rang out from the front of the club. People stampeded from inside, and I disappeared into the darkness. Leaving nothing but bodies behind. Any trace of myself would be lost in the chaos.

The clothes I wore were new, and I'd stored them sealed inside a bag in a locker at the local community center where homeless kept their belongings. The wig I wore was new as were the gloves I wore. I hadn't survived this long without learning how not to leave a piece of myself behind.

A few blocks later, I found a barrel burning and deposited the wig, gloves and facial prosthetics inside. I wrinkled my nose at the scent of burning hair, leather and rubber.

I shoved my hands into the pockets of my jacket and headed to start the next phase of my plan. The phone I used for assignments was tucked inside the inside pocket—turned off so they couldn't trace me. I'd turned it on when I settled

into one of the three buildings I owned. They were all abandoned and falling down, but the perfect place to stash
supplies or hide out.

Cristo would receive my message soon enough. If he
didn't realize the error of his ways, I had more lessons
awaiting and what I'd do to his men, his family, would seem
like a slap on the wrist compared to the hell I'd devised
for him.

My entire body ached from the beatings. They hadn't let me out of the small room. I stared at the peeling wallpaper through one eye. The other had swollen shut the day before. They hadn't started taking fingers or limbs yet, but it was all chaos in the outer room. Voices were getting louder and more panicked as I think two days passed. I'd pass out from the pain and awaken only to be reminded of where I was.

Cowen hadn't come for me, and no one had mentioned him since they'd thrown me in this room. I wanted to cry as I realized that I'd been right and he hadn't rescued me. Part of me wanted to say yet—he hadn't come for me...yet. I didn't know what to do or why they were keeping me alive. I wanted to go home. Cowen kept me safe and happy, nothing was conventional between us, but I wanted it —missed it.

I cried out as the door opened and tried to curl in the corner to make myself smaller.

Cristo, Cowen's former boss, stood in the center of the room; the two men I'd started to think of as the man's enforcers—the ones who took the most pleasure in beating me—waited for the man's orders. I'd heard a couple of names, but the only one I remembered was Cristo's.

"Your man has a way with sending messages. Do you know how many men and women Cowen has killed since I've taken you?"

I didn't bother answering because the last time I'd done it, he'd backhanded me.

"As of an hour ago, he's killed fifteen of my men and their whores. I underestimated his attachment to you. I've messaged him several times to arrange a meet and do you know what he's done, Harrison? Nothing.

"I have to admit, he's smarter than the mindless killer I assumed him to be. He doesn't leave the phone on long enough for us to trace him."

I braced myself as he motioned to one of the men and I had no time to protect myself against the kicks and stomps from steel-toed boots. The pain and impact took my breath away. I was too weak to fight as I was hauled to my feet. My attacker held me against the wall with his hand around my throat.

"Boss, I want to play with him." Foul breath blew in my face as he spoke and he leaned in to stroke his oily cheek over mine.

I cringed and started to fight—I didn't care if I won. I didn't belong to anyone but Cowen. Whether he still wanted me or not, I wasn't going to let this bastard touch me. I'd take every beating, I'd even die gracefully if I needed to, but I wasn't going to let these nasty men anywhere near me. I brought my knee up and grazed the enforcer's crotch, he grunted and slammed my head against the wall. My vision swam, and pain exploded in my head. The constant headache only grew in severity with each beating.

"Someone thinks they have claws, but no, I won't let him have you. You're going to get me Cowen."

I stared out the corner of my eye as I watched the man pull out a phone and start dialing. Cristo pressed the phone to his ear.

"Cowen, I received your messages. I am amazed at your skill. But don't I have something you want?" The phone was suddenly beside my face. "Say hi."

"Cowen? I want to come home—"

"Isn't that sweet, your disposable piece thinks you want him to come home. My boys are having so much fun with him. You have twenty-four hours to make contact. After that, I send him to you a bit at a time."

The call was disconnected, and I sagged against the wall, tears streamed from under my lashes. When my throat was released, I fell to the bare wood floor. My ribs ached, but the pain in my chest was worse. My time was running out. All I had was one more day before they carried through with their threats. I had to believe that Cowen wanted to keep me. He'd gone through so much trouble, and he'd killed for me. Multiple people. They'd taken something that belonged to him, and he was enacting his revenge.

He was a ruthless man. Killing was how he dealt with his problems. I could take a bit of pain if it was just to stay alive until he showed up.

Cristo crouched in front of me and studied me like I was an oddity in a freakshow of old.

"What did you do to make Cowen turn all soft?"

Him implying Cowen was soft forced a laugh out of me. "There's nothing soft about him. He has no empathy. How many jobs has he pulled for you? How many people has he killed for a paycheck?"

"Hundreds. Do you know he killed his parents? Oh,

they can't prove that he'd done so. You wouldn't believe how many people are frightened of him. Assassins with twice as many kills even refused to attempt to take him out. And I tried, they wouldn't even attempt it, and I offered seven-figures for his head."

"If he's as good as you say, why kill him?"

"Because he's a weapon, and sometimes they make a habit of backfiring one day. He's not one to play by the rules. We were never supposed to meet, but I like to know who I'm dealing with."

"You know you're just pissing him off. You did say he killed multiple people in the last two days. What do you think he'll do when you kill me?"

"I'm hoping he's so in love with fucking that ass of yours that it won't come to that."

"He can find another ass to fuck." I was surprised by how evenly I pushed those words through my lips. I didn't like the thought of him replacing me with someone else. Someone else bringing him pleasure. I sensed I was the first one to cause him to lust, and I wanted to it keep it that way. Sharing him wasn't an option for me. He was mine as much as I was his. If, not, when he came for me, I'd make sure he never had a reason to be without me.

I didn't mind dying, yet I didn't want to live without him.

"No, there's something about you Cowen can't resist. We've occasionally watched him over the years, sent in clients just to get a closer look at him. I was told multiple times that he watched you. Why suddenly he felt the need to claim you confuses me. I always believed he was born without a soul. Sold it to the devil for his time here on Earth. No one survives as much as he has to open himself to weakness. I'm not the first one to try to take him out. When you have a dog in the fight, when he gets so aggressive that he can't be controlled, there's only one option, put him down."

I remained silent as I just stared at the man. He actually believed Cowen was some evil spirit aligned with Satan himself. Some people were just born broken, and others were conditioned. I'd seen enough clients, read their files to know some people were just evil. I never thought that about Cowen. He was controlled. Wasn't prone to losing his temper. Every move he made was a calculated and fully planned out maneuver. I'd seen how he handled himself in court, and he never acted impulsively.

Even when he punished me, it was precise and only severe enough to teach me the lesson I needed to learn. I wondered if he'd give me a lesson for not fighting Cristo and his men more. Would he be disappointed in me?

"What are you thinking?"

"Whether he's disappointed in me or not because I didn't try to get away."

"Out of everything, your impending death, or at the very least torture, you're worried if he's disappointed in you?"

I didn't answer because he didn't need to know what relationship Cowen and I had. If he knew I submitted to Cowen's punishment, if they'd taken off my clothes before they started beating me, they would have noticed the bruises on my ass cheeks. The thin, scabbed wounds I'd earned from Cowen's whip. They wouldn't understand, and I wouldn't open myself to them trying it with me. I wasn't into the pain, but I savored it though. The pain showed me Cowen cared about my safety and well-being, that he only wanted me to do better. Cristo and his men would take it as a challenge. I'd seen the way the man in front of me and the guys who worked for him looked at me.

"You are an odd man. You actually believe that you love a killer, that he may love you in return. There's nothing in that man that will ever love. You're just a corpse that doesn't know it's dead yet."

Those were Cristo's last words, and I was left alone as I stared up at the boarded window. The wind whistled through the cracks in the panes. I'd peered out the window after I'd arrived and seen nothing but falling down buildings. From the location, I'd assumed we were in the warehouse district in one of the abandoned hotels near the docks, but I hadn't heard the blaring of horns. I'd checked to see if I could escape, but there was nothing outside the window but a sheer drop.

I curled up on the lumpy, stained mattress, grimacing at what might infest it. I was exhausted and hurt, all I could think about was sleep and when I could go home. Soon, I kept telling myself. He would be there soon, and everything would be put right again.

F or days I'd taken out one person after another, unmerciful to their families, but I'd left mothers and children alive. As much as I wanted to blame all the partners, I didn't see any reason to make the children suffer unduly. I was positioned outside the last house. This was the man who was fourth in command, and I'd leave him alive only long enough to tell me what I needed to know. The ones before him were simply killing for the sake of killing, punishment for what they'd taken from me.

I crossed the street with my head down, and my hands tucked into my pockets at the chill in the air. My mask in place to disguise myself. I had no issues killing the wife, but I'd prefer to leave her alive for an example alone.

The bastard and his wife had entered an hour before, and I could see them sitting in front of their TV having dinner. They were settled and comfortable in the safety of their home. My other marks weren't discovered yet. Cristo had lost control of his crew, or they simply grew complacent because I was one man. Purposely not perceived as a threat and I marveled at their stupidity.

It was my lot in life, my size and looks that made me unremarkable. I was in no way scary in outward appearance. My former employer had forgotten the monster he'd hired. Cristo knew what I was capable of. He'd seen my work many times and had witnessed the cruelty I could inflict without remorse. I loathed everyone except Harrison. I experienced emotions I never had before, and when they'd taken him, the last rein on my control had broken.

The rumors were spreading about the five bodies I'd left at the bar. Did they ignore my warning? My thoughts were Cristo's crew was too stupid to prepare themselves for the war they'd instigated when they'd taken my boy. My rage grew as I imagined what they were doing to him. His body was meant only for my hands—my pain.

I knocked on the door and waited patiently. When the door opened, I slipped my hands from my pocket with my weapon at the ready. Then I placed my suppressor between his eyes.

"Good evening, I hope I'm not interrupting. Oh, yes, I'd love to come in. Back up." I proceeded forward, and the larger man had his hands in the air.

"He's not here."

"I already know that, but what I don't know is where my boy is. I'm surprised Cristo and you all thought it would be prudent to take something from me."

"Haven't you drawn enough blood?"

I would've laughed at the absurdity of his question if I'd known how. I closed the door behind me without taking my attention away from him. "Please inform your wife to make no silly attempts to call the authorities. It'll make it harder on you and her."

When we entered the living room, the woman started to scream and was quickly hushed by her husband. He rushed to her side, and I went to the windows to jerk the curtains together to shield us from the people outside. I had a lot to get done in a short period of time, and disruptions weren't ideal.

"Now, why don't you tell me where my boy is?"

"I'm not telling you shit."

"Not the answer I wanted." I squeezed the trigger and took out his wife's knee, and she screamed. "I take out the other if you don't quiet her now."

The man covered her mouth and quietly whispered in her ear as if to soothe her. It would almost be a sweet display if I didn't know he'd spent the afternoon with a couple of women he fucked at least twice a week. Loyalty was a lost art.

"Where is my boy?"

"You'll never get him back. If they haven't beaten him to death by now, they've used up his ass."

I surged forward and jerked his wife out of his arms. I held her up by her hair and kicked the back of her bad knee to drive her to the floor. I was unused to the rage. I could deal with a lot but my boy made me feel—care, and I didn't understand how to process. Time was running out. Cristo had left messages, and I'd sent ones of my own, but I couldn't allow them to find me first. He would be lost to me because they'd continue to keep him hidden for insurance.

I bent at the waist and pressed my face next to hers and looked at the bastard. It was clear to see he was ready to attack at the smallest opening. "You have a very beautiful wife. How would you feel if I took her from you?"

I drew the silencer down her cheek as I kept eye contact with him. She whimpered so prettily and her face wet with tears brought on by fear and pain.

"You wouldn't dare."

"You'd be surprised at what I'd dare. I've never had anything that belonged to me before. Dying is something I accept as my due for the life I lead, but my boy had nothing to do with it."

"You can't tell Cristo no."

"I'll take her apart piece by piece just as Cristo threatened to do. Where should I start?" I asked as I set my weapon aside and unsheathed my knife.

I placed the tip just below the tender skin beneath her eye. "Maybe something for you and her to remember me by?" I nicked her with the slightest pressure. "Are you going to tell me what I need or do I take the eye first?"

"Fuck, fine, fine. They're hiding in the Beauregard Hotel, near the docks."

I was almost disappointed at how easily he gave in, but I returned my knife to the sheath inside my boot. I picked up my gun. "Do you love your husband?"

"Ye-yes," she stuttered out.

"Tell him."

I slowly raised my arm and aimed.

"I love you."

As soon as the bastard started to open his mouth, I compressed the trigger, and she screamed. She dragged herself to where he was sprawled on the couch. A hole between his eyes. I eased to my feet and stared down at her. She was weeping and holding the corpse of her husband. I grew bored with her blubbering.

"You didn't have to kill him. He told you what you wanted to know."

"You're wrong. His boss needed an example of what I'm capable of because it appears Cristo has forgotten. Would you like to join him?"

"No."

"Remember that, make sure you pass it on to Cristo. If you say anything to anyone, I'll come back. Your only purpose is to make sure Cristo knows there's no one else between him and I. They started this war...I'm simply finishing it."

I left without a backward glance and walked out onto the quiet street. No movement caught my attention—it didn't appear as if anyone was coming to the woman's rescue. I seamlessly disappeared into the shadows and removed my mask as I turned the corner at the end of the block.

The hotel was abandoned. I owned several properties nearby. The buildings were slowly crumbling under years of neglect.

Soon I'd have my boy back where he belonged. I tried not to think about what they were doing to him. My mind needed to be free to focus—to plan. Sirens blared in the distance as I reached my car which I'd parked a mile away. I slipped into the front seat, started the engine and returned to the safe house I'd crashed in since I'd started this operation.

Harrison just needed to hold on a bit longer and then I'd never let him out of my sight. I still didn't understand the power he had over me. I was unused to caring for anyone other than me and most days I rarely cared whether I survived. I wanted him home, curled up in bed beside me, feeling the weight of his larger body. I craved him as if he were an addiction I couldn't break free from. For that reason alone, I should let him go, leave him to whatever fate Cristo had for him. Yet, I couldn't do that. I owned him. His presence was a weakness, but one I'd gladly accept just to have him. When this was over, I'd figure out what made me want him in my life—my bed.

First, I needed to bring him home.

Chapter Twenty

HARRISON

The agony was almost too much. I cried and screamed, begging for them to stop as blows pummeled my ribs as one man beat me and the other two held me against the wall. Cristo was seated calmly on a chair checking his nails and appearing bored.

"We can do this a hundred times. Why make yourself suffer so much over Cowen? I'm quite sure he wouldn't expend the energy on you."

He cared for me, I knew it, and he'd come for me. I dreamed of him until I was rudely awakened for the next round of beatings. They only hit me enough to weaken me, but not enough to break anything, except I felt the bones would give at some point.

"He'll come for me. How many men are you losing in the process?" My voice sounded stronger than I felt. My body weakened from the brutal abuse of the last four days. I was too exhausted to care anymore about what happened to me.

Whatever happened, I knew he'd avenge me at least. I missed him. If someone had told me a few months ago that

I'd have fallen for the man who'd kidnapped me, I would have told them they were crazy. However, with Cowen, I'd found the place I belonged—the one I'd looked for most of my life.

I was tossed to the floor, and I curled there on my side trying to control my breathing. As long as I didn't move, I didn't hurt as much. The taste of blood filled my mouth from what I assumed was a cut to the inside of my lip or cheek.

"This hero of yours is a depraved psychopath. He cares for no one except himself. Why are you so confident that he'll break a sweat finding you?"

"Because I belong to him."

"Like a possession? Oh, but those can be replaced easy enough. The first job I contracted Cowen to do, I needed information extracted. He skinned the poor bastard alive. There wasn't enough left on his body to do grafts. He died of sepsis in the hospital several days after they found him discarded like trash on the street."

I didn't know why he kept telling me stories as if I didn't know what Cowen could do. He'd never lied to me about the type of man he was. I knew he could wield a whip as a weapon to punish me. Yet, I also knew what it felt like when he fucked me. I loved his commanding nature. The fact he didn't hide who he truly was, maybe I'd never be truly comfortable with a man who killed for a living—pleasure.

All I knew was I wanted to go home.

"I know who he is."

"You don't know shit. One day he'll turn on you and what happens then, Harrison? Do you think the man who is incapable of love will show you a second of mercy? No, he will destroy you, and the only thing you can hope for is he makes it quick.

"He's killed my entire crew...the only remaining members are in this building. He took out all of them," Cristo yelled as he surged to his feet.

I forced my body to move to put more distance between us. It didn't matter if I could protect myself. At least I could delay the inevitable. I was shocked they'd kept me around as long as they had. Each day they came to me with another update of the men Cowen had taken out. Tonight was different though. No matter how calm Cristo appeared, he had a wild look in his eyes. Like an animal turning feral at being backed into a corner.

If it were true and Cowen had killed his entire crew, then the only men standing between us were the ones protecting the building. Hope flared at what that could mean. He'd come soon to take me home. Also, a sense of dread tempered my optimism. Cowen was one man against what could be a small army of men.

The thought of him getting hurt made my chest hurt. I could lose him so easily. I really must be losing it if I was more worried about the professional assassin than I was about myself. The minute Cowen entered the building, they could kill me out of spite.

Cristo crouched in front of me and his cold smile made me nauseous.

"I'm looking forward to the look on his face when I kill you. I want him to see the moment I take his most valuable possession from him. It's said that your man can't feel pain. We'll find out if that's true when he sees the life leave your eyes and knows it's all his fault."

Cristo pushed to his feet, thankfully he left and took his enforcers with him. I lay on the floor trying to get my bearings. Was that the plan all along? To lure Cowen here only to kill me when he came? I stayed on the floor hurting and depressed as I saw the life I'd started to look forward to slip away.

I hadn't thought that being with Cowen would be easy. The man killed people for a living, and when he wasn't doing that, he defended people in court. I wasn't going to make it to my thirtieth birthday. Maybe I'd accepted Cowen too easily. I still liked someone else taking charge, I loved that it was Cowen. I just didn't know—processing it was difficult. And I felt guilty for questioning my feelings for him, and maybe I should be admitting what it was, I'd formed an unnatural attachment to my kidnapper.

A series of pops I was sure were gunfire had me jerking to a sitting position, and my ribs screamed in pain. Men started yelling, and Cristo's was loudest among them. He barked orders and told the men out there to shoot to kill. I struggled to my feet. As soon as I was steady, the door opened, and Cristo was charging toward me.

He wrapped his arm around my neck and pulled me back to his chest. I awkwardly stumbled out of the room with his body pushing me. He positioned us directly across from the door with his gun pressed to my head.

"I knew he'd come for you. He might not give a fuck about you, but I took something that was his. He couldn't fucking resist retrieving his property."

"He'll kill me before he lets you have me."

"I doubt that. The cold bastard might have a heart and want to keep you. Wouldn't that be novel, the depraved murderer getting soft."

I blocked out what he was mumbling. His voice had risen several octaves sounding almost deranged. The man was mad, and I no longer knew what he planned or even if he had one. The chaos intensified outside the battered door.

The screams and shouts became louder. There was a war out there, and in my gut, I knew Cowen was unstoppable.

He didn't possess fear or empathy—he'd destroy anyone in his wake, and he wouldn't stop until someone did it for him. I couldn't suppress my tears or terror any longer. As soon as Cowen entered the room, they'd take him out. I took in the men on either side of the door just waiting for the moment to strike Cowen down.

The booming sounds of gunfire made me flinch as I pictured Cowen laying in a bloody heap and then the door flew open. Cowen stood there in all black. There was a deadness to his eyes and then his gaze met mine.

"Boy, are you okay?" he asked, and his voice was almost soft with that edge of caring he used after he finished with my lessons.

"Y—yes, sir." I lied so as not to distract him. If he did care, I didn't want him worried about me.

"Cowen, so glad you could join us," Cristo replied as if he'd invited Cowen over for dinner and wasn't holding a gun to my head.

"I could've forgiven your attempts to kill me, but you took my boy. That I can't forget."

"Your boy is very...sweet."

I held my breath as he raised his arm in slow motion and watched as Cowen pulled the trigger. Everything in me froze at that moment, and the spell was only broken as Cristo screamed in pain. Instead of releasing me, the man braced his weight on me as he favored his injured leg.

"You sonofabitch!"

After that, it was chaos and Cowen was in a battle for our lives and I was too useless to help. It was two against one, and I was waiting for Cristo to tire of the scene playing out in front of us and use his gun to strike Cowen down.

Chapter Twenty-One

COWEN

They were so confident. I watched from my position on the roof a few buildings away from where they held my boy. I'd taken out several of Cristo's enforcers, but I had kept one alive long enough to tell me what I needed to know. I'd listened to the last message Cristo had left. My boy telling me he wanted to come home had caused my stomach to do a strange thing. He sounded so lost, and I'd hated it, but I needed to take down everyone who could carry on Cristo's operation or scare them enough as I tortured their whores, wives, husbands, partners.

I had made it my mission to destroy Cristo, and now it was time to end it. I'd scanned the building by infrared and figured out they kept my boy in a corner bedroom on the northeast side of the dilapidated hotel. Parts of the city were rundown and abandoned, shadows of their former grandeur. The foundation of this city was built by prohibition, gangsters, and speakeasies.

There would always be someone to carry on history, but it wouldn't be Cristo.

For most of my adult life, I observed the world through the scope of my rifle. Mentally I tagged each target as I found them roaming the roof and balconies, waiting for me. Their faces lined with exhaustion from the days of war I'd subjected them. Just like with the men who'd tried to assassinate me before, they'd underestimated their target.

I pressed the butt of the gun comfortably against my shoulder, the rough texture of the stock touched my cheek. The world shrunk down to fit in the view of my scope. Nothing existed outside this moment—the kill. My heart beat a steady, easy rhythm and the pace of my breaths were deep and even. It didn't require emotion, just a steady hand and the will to do what I found necessary. I aimed my scope at the room I assumed Harrison resided. The windows were cracked and the night was chilly, and I wondered if he was cold. I inhaled as I found one of the guards on the roof. The man was hidden from view from the others by the roof access. As I'd done hundreds of times before, I exhaled and squeezed the trigger. The silencer muffled the sound. The man's head exploded as I hit him between his eyes.

I efficiently ejected the cartridge, loaded, and took out the other three without alerting anyone. There was a reason they compensated me well for my work. I didn't give into second thoughts.

Pausing, I made sure the coast was clear and no one else appeared from the propped open door. I had two hours between guard changes, but I didn't need that much time. The people I'd already taken out were considered Cristo's inner circle, except for two of his most trusted. They never left his side. Setting my weapon aside, I jumped to my feet and bent to pick my rifle back up. On my way to the fire escape, I slung the strap over my shoulder and stepped over the edge. I jogged down to the street below. I opened the trunk, stowed my rifle inside, armed myself with a blade and added extra magazines into the holders on my flak jacket. I checked and rechecked the twin 9mms and returned one to my thigh holsters.

It was time to get my boy back and take care of Cristo and the rest of his crew. The shadows concealed my approach. I'd only counted eleven heat signatures inside the building, and I'd eliminated four of them on the roof. *Only six to go.* I checked the scene and saw no one, so taking advantage, I jogged across the street. As soon as I was back in the shadows cast by the building, I hugged the wall and slowly made my way to the front entrance.

I raised my arms and extended them, then made entry. The information extracted from the man I'd briefly kept alive gave me a rough outline of positions. They seemed to stay close to where they kept my boy.

There was a skinny guy posted next to the elevators. He automatically reached for his gun when I pressed the barrel of mine at the base of his skull.

"Now, you don't want to make this more painful than necessary. Throw it away."

"You're outnumbered you know that, right?"

I didn't bother answering as I kept a close watch on him as he leaned slightly to the side and dropped the gun, kicking it several feet away. I rested my free hand on his shoulder.

"Push the button."

"You're going to die here."

"Maybe, but you'll draw your final breath before I will."

I kept the bastard as a shield while we waited for the elevator to descend. When the door opened, a man stood inside. His shock made him slow to draw his weapon, and I fired once.

"Motherfucker," my shield screamed when I squeezed the trigger right next to his ear.

I shoved him forward and shifted to put my back to the rear of the car. I peeked around him to make sure he hit the right floor. As we ascended, I mentally prepared myself for the coming firefight. I'd taken precautions to take out the easiest targets first. All the men left were the ones guarding my boy and the bastard in front of me.

Calm came over me. I'd done this hundreds of times before. A few more bodies wouldn't stain my soul if I was wrong about the afterlife. Unlike the kills of my past, the last few days were about getting my boy back. I'd waited a long time to find someone to call mine. They'd made the mistake of thinking they could take him from me.

The old elevator shuddered as it came to a stop and the sliding panels opened. I pushed the man forward and heard shots ring out. Curses came from either end of the corridor.

After that, my every action was choreographed. Yells rang out to announce my arrival like the gunfire wouldn't have alerted the others. I crouched down, keeping the panels open. I took down the guard in the hallway to my left. He shouted in agony, and I barely flinched at the round that hit my vest right on my shoulder blade. I spun and fell to my side, taking out the guy on the right. I grunted as shots rang out wildly and a few hit my chest.

I jumped to my feet and followed the plans I memorized until I reached the suite where my boy was being kept. With a single kick, the door swung open, and I trained my gun right on Cristo. He was using my boy as cover. Harrison's face was streaked with tears. The bruises, cuts, and swollen eye caused my rage to break free, even as I tried to control it. Not only had they dared take him from me, they'd put their hands on him.

"Boy, are you okay?"

"Y—yes, sir," he lied to me as he shook his head to tell me he was hurt.

"Cowen, so glad you could join us."

"I could've forgiven your attempts to kill me, but you took my boy. That I can't forget."

"Your boy is very...sweet."

I aimed, exhaled, and compressed the trigger hitting the toe of his expensive, left shoe. He screamed, and I felt satisfaction.

"You sonofabitch!"

He didn't release Harrison, instead used my boy as a crutch to keep him on his feet. Too much of him was hidden behind Harrison. As I was about to take out his kneecap next, I caught a blur in the corner of my eye and ducked and rolled just in time. One of Cristo's enforcers tried to take my head off with a bat. The gun slipped from my hand and skittered across the floor. I drew my blade and gained my feet again.

"We can forget all about this, Cowen. I must say you impressed me with your skills the last few days."

Cristo's voice was slurred and broken with pain. I kept my focus on the enforcer as he was joined by another man, bigger than the first.

Then I made my first mistake, Harrison cried out in pain, and I jerked my head around to check on him. As soon as I did, the two men were on me. I fought for myself, for my boy, I took hits and kicks, but they never got me to the ground. The bigger of my opponents went down as I caught the side of his throat with my blade. The warmth of blood splashed across my face, and I quickly swiped my forearm across my eyes.

I felt the sharp stab against my ribs and looked down in

time to see my opponent's bloody knife appear from beneath my vest. I felt nothing. He stared into my eyes, a smirk tugged at the corner of his mouth. His arrogance proved his downfall. I grabbed the back of his head, flexed and feigned right, as I brought my knee up to shatter his ribs. He fell face first as he lay prone on the floor as I severed his spinal cord.

Cristo took the coward's way and fired, but his aim was ruined by panic and pain. The shots hit my vest, and as I approached, his gun jammed. He shoved my boy to the floor. Desperately the man tried to clear the chamber but didn't make it in time to save himself.

The wall I pushed him against cracked, then gave under his weight. I stalked to him and dropped to one knee where he'd sagged to the floor.

"Now, what were you saying?"

"Price isn't a problem, name it."

"You think I want money. No, Cristo. We made a deal, when I was done, I was done. You came for me through my boy. You touched him. I can't let that go unpunished." I grabbed the hand he used to touch my boy. I placed the blade at the base of his index finger and severed it. "I'm going to take each piece of you that touched him."

"Sir, please, I wanna go home."

I removed two more before I looked at Harrison.

"Did he rape you, boy?"

"No, sir."

I turned my attention back to Cristo. "You're not as stupid as I thought you were. Any more deals and offers?"

"You can't do th—"

His words ended in a scream as I cut through his femoral artery and he grabbed his crotch. It was useless to try to stop the bleeding. He'd be dead in a matter of minutes. I straightened, and the adrenaline of the fight started to ebb.

I approached my boy and held out my hand. "Let's go home and get you cleaned up. I need a doctor to check you over."

I stumbled as I became dizzy, but I shook it off. I helped him downstairs and over two blocks to where the car waited. He refused to look at me. He understood that the assumption of the violence I was capable of was one thing. Seeing it was another. Carefully I buckled him into the passenger seat and made the call to a doctor I knew who'd make a house call if the price was right.

The blood that was quickly wetting my pants told me I needed to see him myself, but my boy came first.

Chapter Twenty-Two

HARRISON

The doctor left an hour before with strict instructions to keep an eye on Cowen. The man had taken care of my own stitches and checked to make sure I didn't have any permanent damage. Cowen had made a call to the stranger minutes before he'd collapsed. I hadn't noticed he was bleeding until it was almost too late. I'd thought about what his so-called job entailed, but until he'd rescued me, I hadn't understood just how dangerous the persona was that Cowen kept beneath the surface.

He hadn't flinched when he killed one man after another, but what had scared me the most was he hadn't cared about what happened to his body. The rounds he'd taken to the vest hadn't slowed him down. The thrusts of knives and hits from all sides were brushed off as if he were just shooing away an annoying bug.

Could I stay with the knowledge one day he might not come home? He seemed uncaring about his safety while putting me above him. I didn't like it. I'd lost my mother, and I couldn't lose anyone else. Especially when that person had so quickly become my center—my weird comfort.

He started to thrash in his sleep, and I acted without thought. I ran my fingers through his sweaty hair. He didn't allow me to touch him often. He appeared to calm. It brought back too many memories of watching my mother waste away and how helpless I'd been to help her.

I checked the bottles of pills the doctor left. One he'd told me was for pain and another to help fight infection. The doctor hadn't offered to come back, and I figured the visit wasn't really legal. I snorted at the thought. Of course it wasn't legal, Cowen killed people for a living. He couldn't really go to the hospital with impact bruises from multiple gunshots or the knife wound that had barely missed his liver.

"What if I just ran?" I asked myself as I straightened to go get bottles of water for him.

A surprisingly firm grip circled my wrist. "I'd prefer not to kill you."

I let him pull me down to sit beside him on the bed. "Be still my heart, you're so romantic."

"I never claimed to be." His voice was weak and gruffer with pain.

It worried me. He was always so capable and untouchable. The sight of him in assassin mode had transfixed me. I had to admit for a brief moment I'd thought him bad-boy sexy.

"You are rather sexy when you're beating people up."

I wanted to place my hands on his chest, face, somewhere but I didn't know where. If I hurt him, I wouldn't be able to handle it. Caring for him had made me forget about my own pain. I ached over every inch of my body. I could no longer open my left eye, not even to peek beneath the swollen lid. The doctor had checked me over after he'd examined Cowen. Bruised and banged up, but nothing appeared to be broken. I'd been the lucky one, and I needed to focus on him. The physical effects would fade soon enough.

"No one has ever said I was sexy before."

"You're too scary for people to approach. I think I'm going to take advantage of you being off your game for a bit."

"I never forget anything. I'll keep a tally of lashes."

"Of course you will. I'm going to go grab you some water so you can take your pain pills."

"Don't need—"

"Quit being tough."

"I'm not. I don't feel pain like normal people."

I frowned and realized I didn't know much about Cowen's past. We existed in the present.

"Why do you do all this?"

"I'm good at it."

"Cowen, it has to be more than you being good at it. From what I can tell from your win rate, you're an amazing lawyer."

"Assassins need backup plans."

He didn't expand on what that meant. I wondered if he'd ever grow to trust me.

"I'm supposed to trust in you, so why won't you talk to me about your life?"

"Do you want to know that I killed my first psychiatrist when I found out he was going to commit me as a danger to society? Maybe when I made my parents disappear. They'd become frightened of me when I was no more than a toddler. I was...broken. I've never felt anything but the need to kill for as long as I can remember. And I remember everything."

Those were the most words I'd ever heard him speak at

one time. Even though he said he didn't feel pain, I could see the strain in his thin face. I figured anyone else would be screaming in agony from their wounds. He wasn't so I didn't push the meds, but I wanted him to keep talking even if I knew he needed his rest to get better.

"You want to keep me, though?"

"Yes."

"Why?"

"I don't know. Solving problems is all I've ever enjoyed. You're an enigma. My fascination didn't wane after being in your company. You didn't bore me."

"I guess that's good."

He wasn't a sweet talker, and I didn't hold my breath waiting for him to confess some undying love. I doubted I would ever hear him say it—even if he felt it. Emotion was an abstract concept to him. While locked in the basement and spending time with him, I realized he spent time analyzing everything, every word or action needed to be broken down to a molecular level—even me.

"When you became a witness, I couldn't kill you. Taking lives is simple for me. I was going to play with you. Test my hypotheses on why you were different. As I watched you, the more days to pass, I became unwilling to let you go."

"While I'm happy to be alive and that you changed your mind, what happens when you're no longer fascinated with me? Do you still plan to kill me?"

"You're the only person I stopped wanting to kill. I will keep you. Never run from me. There's nowhere you could hide."

I didn't know why that made me smile, but I figured that's as close as he was going to get to admitting he cared for me.

"I need you to be honest with me. Don't hide. This thing between us isn't normal."

"It's all I have to offer."

"All I need is your honesty."

"I've killed hundreds of people. Barely tolerate the human species, but I can't imagine not having you."

That's romantic in a twisted way. I leaned down until my mouth hovered over his. "May I have a kiss?" My busted ribs screamed with pain, and I barely held myself up when my body threatened to collapse.

"Your lips are busted." His slender hand stroked over my bearded cheek, and his thumb skimmed the cuts on my lips.

"Then be gentle."

"I don't know how."

I didn't think that was true. He'd shown me how tender he could be when he cared for me after my lessons and he bathed me. He knew who he was, but his perception of himself was skewed by living in his head. Unlike me, I'd seen glimpses of a different man. Yes, he had his sadistic moments. His infliction of pain more comfortable than giving pleasure. Although all the times we'd had sex, he'd never left me wanting, except when orgasm denial was used as discipline.

"I can show you." I barely pressed my lips to his, but I didn't linger. "I'm going to take a shower, and then I'm going to give you a sponge bath. You're a bit of a mess."

"Do you find me...attractive?"

Did I? The angles of his face were too harsh. His body was littered with scars and missing flesh. But I loved how the smaller man made me feel when he wanted me.

"Others have found me disgusting."

"You're not disgusting. Scars just showed you survived. Get some sleep...I'll be back soon."

He nodded and closed his eyes, but I knew he wouldn't sleep. In all the time I'd spent with him since he'd moved me upstairs, I hadn't noticed him sleep more than a few hours. I eased up off the bed. I felt grimy after days of not bathing and the dried blood on my skin. A long, hot shower would do my aching muscles good. Then I could tend to him, bathe him and change the bloody sheets. First, I needed to take care of myself.

~~~

I WAS EXHAUSTED; SIX DAYS OF WORRY PUSHED ME closer to the edge of collapse. My poor man kept spiking a fever, and I'd have to cool him down. Getting him to take the pills the doctor left was a fight I barely won. I'd found it nearly impossible to keep the man in bed.

His stitches hadn't survived his stubbornness. I'd found butterfly bandages in his first-aid kit and made do with those. Finally, the skin was knitted back together and left a thick, ridge of irritated scar tissue. He was absolutely the worst patient. I pushed his sweaty hair back from his forehead and stretched out beside him. I was too tired to sleep, but I'd discovered I loved watching him. Guilt plagued me as I took advantage of his weakened state. I spread my right hand over his smooth pectorals and reveled in the softness of his skin. His body was so different from my hairier one.

I traced every scar I could reach, even the deep valleys that he'd explained were from an explosion a former boss had used to take him out. He talked about someone trying to murder him as if the man had simply tried to fire him. I shook my head as the sheet across his hips started to jerk as his cock responded to my touch.

"You're not up to it."

"Boy, you're not in charge here."

"Y—yes, sir." My pulse increased as he slapped my bare hip and the sting sent chills over my body. He shifted on the bed, and seconds later he placed our lube in my hand.

"Suck me while you stretch yourself."

Resistance didn't cross my mind as he threw the sheet from his body. Too many days had passed since I'd felt sir inside me. I was helpless when he used that dominating, guttural voice. I knelt between his legs, slicked my fingers, and quickly swallowed his dick, choking on it in my haste. While I sucked every thick inch to the back of my throat, I started to work my fingers into my hole. I shivered at the burning pressure.

"My boy got greedy."

I whined in answer as my jaw quickly started to ache trying to take the girth. The wet, suckling sounds filled my ears joining the rhythmic rushing of blood. Spit ran from the corners of my lips. I gave it to him rough and sloppy just like I knew he liked. When I gagged around the fat head, he urged me on with a deep gravely rumble.

"Fuck, boy." He growled and grabbed the back of my head forcing my face into his groin.

I couldn't breathe or move. At his roughness, the muscles of my ass clenched around the three fingers I was shoving brutally past the resistance. He finally gave me a reprieve. He jerked me off his cock, and I tried to take him back into my mouth, but his hold on my hair kept me restrained.

"Open your fucking mouth and stick out your tongue."

I did as he ordered without question, and he laid his cockhead on my tongue and stroked in savage strokes.

"I should punish you for what you do to me."

I yelped as he released his dick and he smacked my cheek once, twice and a third time until the side of my face was on fire. He shoved my face against his balls. The scent of him strong and I tried to nuzzle closer to his smooth sac. I should protest, fight him, but my cock only got harder at his feral actions.

Quickly he shoved me away, and I stared at him, thinking he was done playing with me.

"Present your ass for me."

I was shaking with nerves. I'd seen him in a lot of moods, but something was different. I rolled over, rested my cheek on the bed and opened my cheeks to show him my hole. Seconds drew out, but I didn't move, and then a scream tore out of my throat as he shoved the firm dildo that he'd bought me inside without warning. I dropped my hands to the bed and fisted them in the sheet. I cried and tried to relax as he used the toy on me, brutally without care.

The erection I had fled quickly and then the toy was gone, and the heat of his thick, long dick was sliding in with absolute care. He deeply groaned. A sigh slipped between my lips as his hips met my hairy ass. He spread his hands across my lower back. The gentleness in comparison to the ferocity of minutes before shocked my system and tears leaked from under my lashes.

It was different—he loved on my ass in long strokes. My dick was hard again and the wet tip laid on the curve of my belly.

"Boy."

I whimpered as he changed angles and aimed for my

gland, I didn't know what to do. How to react, his loving was always rough. I buried my face in the mattress as his calloused hand encircled my cock and jacked me in a pace that matched his hips.

"Does my boy like it when I'm gentle or—" He slammed forward, and I grunted.

He retreated in a slow, smooth movement, then slammed forward. It was an agonizing sensation to be empty. I was made to be full of him.

"I'm going to cum, sir."

"Not until I say you do. Do I own you?"

"Yes, sir. Always."

"I own your pleasure. You don't cum without my permission. You were fucking made for me."

The intensity of his possession built from loving to the brutal fucking I loved. I lifted my ass higher. My cock repeatedly slapped on my belly. His dirty talk embarrassed me even as he was balls deep.

"My shy boy knows how to take my cock. Show me, boy."

I didn't hesitate as I rocked my hips at a frantic speed as I measured his cock. Our bodies were slamming together. He spanked my hips as I took his cock until my flesh burned with the abuse. Agony and ecstasy coalesced until my release ripped through my balls and seed covered my belly. I yelled as he was gone and I turned to find him staring at me, his gaze cold.

"I'm sorry, sir, I didn't—"

He was positioned in front of me, and he held my chin in a hard grip.

"You didn't listen. Therefore, you don't earn my cum in your ass."

I cried at his disappointment as he held his cock in front

of my face, stroking it as he stared at me with anger. I didn't have time to react before his cum covered my face. Everything inside me froze as he removed his touch and presence and I heard the bathroom door close. I knelt in the middle of the bed, staring at the dark stained wood and waited.

It seemed like forever until I heard the shower stop and he opened the door. The water still running in the bathroom. He was naked with his dark hair slicked back from his face.

"I'm sorry."

"When I tell you to do something, boy, you listen. This isn't just about your pleasure. You trust me to know how to keep you happy and safe."

He gently cleaned my face, watching me, and I noticed his face looked softer. His body wasn't tense as if on guard.

"Yes, sir."

"I don't want to lose you."

Before I could answer, he kissed me, then helped me off the bed. He led me to the bathroom where he was filling the tub. I let him take care of me. I barely kept my eyes open as he washed and tended to me. Cleaning my ass with soft strokes inside and out. I enjoyed the dichotomy of his viciousness and tenderness, and he always made sure that I was given everything I needed.

COWEN

W e were back to the real world of the cabin and penthouse. I observed Harrison closer over the days since we'd recovered enough to come out of hiding. The few clients I had, I'd transferred to other lawyers in the city using the excuse of being in an accident. The breaks healed and the bruises faded, and it was time to get back to work. I'd taken a freelance job or two, and I didn't like that I had to be away from Harrison. I'd decided this was my last for a while. We needed some time to rebuild the trust between us that was broken when he was taken from me.

I'd noticed my unusual attachment to him had intensified. When he was out of my sight, I worried and wondered if he was safe. I kept an eye on the cameras I had in both our homes. His safety had become more important than either of my jobs. I didn't know what it was or how to describe the emotions I felt for my boy. It bordered on obsessive.

Attachment of any kind was the downfall for a man like me. Didn't Cristo taking Harrison from me prove that it was safer to set him free? The thought pained me. I still felt no

remorse or empathy for anyone or anything, except for him.
I still punished him when he broke my rules. I loved on and
fucked him several times a day.

He begged for my whip or flogger. He was the perfect
counter for my depraved nature. He was sweet and...loving,
I could see the odd emotions in his gaze when I found him
watching me. Someone loved me, even knowing what and
who I was. He had no reservations about telling me repeatedly that he was mine. I didn't know how to keep him. My
own parents couldn't get rid of me fast enough, and I hadn't
given a second thought to the moment I killed them. I felt it
was only a matter of time that he went the way of everyone
else in my life who claimed to care.

I'd taken care of my job—they wanted a public execu-
tion. I'd eliminated my target as he'd given a speech about
some monstrosity of steel and glass, and then I'd laid low for
a few days before starting the twelve-hour trip home. I
called or texted him every hour or two, just to hear his voice.

I'd made him lie in our bed and get off as I listened to
him on the phone, watched him on my laptop. My cock
ached thinking about him, and I was helpless to resist him. I
was suddenly a slave to my body's response to him. He
never protested—always so quick to submit.

I connected the call to him.

"Are you on your way home?"

"Does my boy miss me?"

"Yes, sir."

"Have you been fucking yourself with your toys without
my permission?"

"Yes, sir, you know I have. You watch me on the
cameras."

I was shocked by the pull at the corners of my mouth as
he made me smile. The first few times it happened I'd had

to stare into the mirror as the lines beside my eyes deepened, and I looked almost normal. His bratty behavior should anger me, but I knew why he did it. He willfully disobeyed me just so I would take him in hand.

"How was your business trip?"

It surprised me that he asked about my work as if it was any other out of town business meeting. "Successful."

"As always. Did you get me a present?"

"Do you think you deserve one after giving yourself orgasms? Do I need to start making you wear your cock cage again when I'm away?"

"No, sir, you know I don't like it."

"It's punishment, boy, you're not supposed to like it."

I heard his disgruntled little huff and knew exactly what he looked like when he did it. The way his full lips became poutier. I remember every bad thing in my life, the face of every victim. The ability to remember anything and everything had always seemed more of a curse than a blessing. That was until I'd met Harrison.

"You're quiet. Have you been eating and sleeping?"

"You're not around to take care of me, boy."

"When are you going to be home? I can make you something to eat."

I still didn't enjoy food or anything, it was just something I had to do to survive, but I ate and slept because it made my boy happy. While I took care of him, guided him when needed, he took pride in taking care of me as well.

"I'll be home in about six hours, and this will be my last trip for a while."

"Really, sir, are you sure?"

"I feel that I need to stay close to home. You've been displaying some anxiety and having nightmares. We need to rebuild trust and get you grounded. I can't do that while I'm away."

"I'd like that, sir."

I heard the honesty in his words. He liked it when I was around. He sought me for comfort, even if it was just to place his head on my knee as I worked at home or in the office. When I'd order him to suck my cock, he greedily did as I said. When he was anxious, I let him suck to soothe himself like a boy sucking his thumb to fall asleep. His head resting on my thigh and I'd run my fingers through his soft hair. He asked for so little, and I thought I didn't have enough to keep him happy, but every day he proved me wrong.

"I want you to go get ready, bathe, stretch yourself and put your plug in and be waiting in our bed for me when I get home."

"Yes, sir."

"Is my slutty boy ready for his sir's cock?"

A broken moan filled the interior of my car.

"Yes, sir. The toys you bought me don't fill my ass like you do."

"And they never will. Be ready, boy."

I disconnected the call and opened the app for the cameras to make sure my boy was getting ready for me. He was naked per my rules. He was never to wear clothes in our homes. I should always have access to him. He never denied me. He was always prepped and stretched with a plug in when we were at home, and sometimes I even made him wear it at work. If I wanted to fuck my boy, I didn't want to wait to be balls deep in his ass.

He was never to hide from me. I demanded him to be vocal even in the office. I didn't care if someone came in and knew I was using my boy. I owned every inch of him. As far as I was concerned, he'd be mine until one of us drew our last breath. I was just unsure of how to tell him that. I knew the words that were expected. I'd just never said them before, these odd feelings I had had to mean I loved him.

I'd tried to say it so many times, but the words always stuttered on the tip of my tongue. I'd never felt insecure about anything, I'd accepted myself for how I was born, but he made me want to be different for him. The rest of the world didn't matter to me. I didn't care what anyone thought of me except him. I wondered if he felt similarly to me, but he showed me he was mine—that he cared, but he'd yet to confess more in words. It was all in his acts of submission and care.

Love was such an odd concept. To feel more for someone than you do for yourself. That you put someone's happiness and comfort ahead of your own. I'd taken him to study the strangeness of humanity. To analyze emotional clues and in doing so, I'd opened myself to something beyond my own embraced depravity. Yes, I caused him pain, but only to teach him, to let him know that I cared about his safety. I fucked him because his actions showed me that he needed my possession. The satisfaction I received from providing for him was almost as fulfilling as owning his body.

I wanted to give him something to show him that he was mine. On the trip home, I debated what would be perfect for him. In my gut, I knew he'd appreciate whatever reward I gave him. I was in strange territory. I was still lost and confused about the newness, and my brain refused to stop analyzing it. Decades of habit weren't wiped away in a matter of weeks or months. Before Harrison, my life was simple. It was all about the kill and keeping the halves of my life separated.

He changed that. He existed on both sides. The first person I'd trusted and the possibility of his betrayal loomed. Hope was an alien thing, but part of me tried to reach for it —hold onto it. I refused to give him up. I'd killed for him and would do so again if the need called for it.

I pulled off onto an exit to stop for gas and then I would get straight home to my boy.

Chapter Twenty-Four

HARRISON

Cowen was making me nervous. He was normally quiet, but he'd grown even more silent over the weeks. His security measures tightened with extra cameras and sensors. When he asked what I wanted for a reward, I'd told him that I wanted to come back to the diner.

I tried not to laugh at the stiffness of his body as if he were waiting for an attack or more aptly to attack. He wouldn't even touch the menu.

"You promised."

"Boy, I said I'd take you to dinner. I did not say I would enjoy it."

I was about to pout until Freda came to the table.

"Do you know how worried I was?" Freda fussed and was about to cuff me on the back of the head until Cowen cleared his throat.

When we were out together, he always put himself between me and other people. No one was ever given the opportunity to touch me. "I'm sorry. I just needed time to myself." I'd told the lie enough that it came easily to me.

"I see you found yourself a young man while you were away."

She started to hug me, and the sound of him making that sound in his throat grew louder. She didn't seem to pick up on it and gave me her usual embrace she reserved for regulars. I'd missed coming here. When my mother passed away, this had become the place where I could spend an hour or two just to feel less alone.

"Freda, Cowen, Cowen, Freda."

"Your asshole boss?"

I shot a glance at him just in time to catch the lift of one of his heavy brows and the look he gave me promised punishment later.

"He's nicer than I first thought." The lesson I'd get when we returned home flashed through my mind, and I shivered. It had nothing to do with fear.

"Your usual, what about you?" she asked him.

"Same."

"Oh...kay. I'll be right back with drinks." She picked up the menus and left us alone.

"Be nice, please."

"In our long acquaintance, when have I shown that I was nice? Apparently, you always assumed I was an asshole."

I tried to pick out the nuances in his tone which were absent or subtle. In this case, he gave nothing away. Freda returned with our drinks, and I nodded my thanks, then waited for her to leave again.

"You've been very nice to me."

"I enjoy fucking my boy."

I darted my gaze around the room to make sure no one was paying attention. I sometimes forgot Cowen didn't know how to deal with regular people. I brought my attention back to him, and he seemed completely unfazed. Elegant in his three-piece suit in the middle of a diner filled with people in jeans and t-shirts. His spine and shoulders straight as he studied me in that way which made me feel as if no one else existed for him but me. Although, I knew better. He was always on guard.

He reached inside his jacket and removed a wooden jeweler box with the logo of the most exclusive boutique in the city. They didn't sell anything below a five-digit price tag. He set the box on the table and slid it toward me.

"What is it?"

"Open it."

I eased it open, the hinge making the slightest creaking sound. Inside a bed of silk rested a cuff bracelet. Staring at it, I realized what it was. It was a perfectly detailed whip cuff that would encircle my wrist several times.

"What is this?"

"I've owned you since the minute you stepped into my office. Now I want you to wear my ownership."

"What does it mean?"

"It means that you're mine until the end of our days on this cesspool of a planet."

I lifted my present from the box and tested the textures under the pads of my thumbs. Cowen had told me plenty that he owned me—that I was his, but this seemed so much more tangible. Something I could touch and look at, a gift that would only have meaning to the two of us.

"Okay."

"I don't think I asked if you agreed or not."

"You're losing romance points."

"Is that a thing?"

The confusion was clear on his face, and I hid my expression from him so he wouldn't see me smiling at him.

He wasn't the greatest with emotional queues, and he'd probably interpret it wrong. My man was clueless as to how to be human, and I'd accepted that. I wanted Cowen more than I wanted conventional. It wasn't roses or candlelit dinners. Oh, he'd give them to me if I asked, but just like him bringing me to the diner, he didn't like or understand any of it. I had to take the good with the bad, the killer, and the clueless man.

"Put it on me, please."

He took it when I held it out for him. It easily flexed to slip over my hand. It almost appeared too fragile to wear—hidden in the hair on my wrist and forearm. He surprised me when he kissed the backs of my fingers. I was rewarded with a flash of possessiveness in his usually impassive eyes. He didn't talk about his feelings or what was going on in his head as freely as I'd like. Yet his actions always showed he cared for me.

Sometimes I wished he'd say the L-word. That would probably be a gift he'd never give me. Only for the fact that love didn't have a tangible feeling for him to grasp. It was a complex mixture of emotions he couldn't break down into facets he could analyze with his five senses.

"I love you, too."

The utter shock on his handsome face amazed me. I wonder if anyone had ever said it to him. The stories he'd told me of his parents weren't filled with unconditional love or affection. They were too frightened of their child to offer him platitudes of familial love. He may believe he was born broken. A product that never should've survived to birth, but his upbringing didn't help the bad wiring.

I could say I love you enough for the both of us. I knew our time together was probably limited. I'd seen his other life and how easy it would be for him not to come home. My mother's death, while tragic, had taught me lessons in life, and the most important one was we weren't guaranteed years to come. Cherishing what time we did have, not waiting to be hit with the what-ifs later on.

He seemed about to speak, but Freda showed up, placing plates in front of us. He snarled his nose at what he was being served, meatloaf and mashed potatoes was the ultimate in comfort food, add cheesecake to the meal, and I was happy.

"Enjoy."

"Thanks." I started to eat and noticed he was staring at his plate. "I'd like to keep you around, and in order to do that, you need food."

"I'm only eating because my body requires sustenance. It's the twenty-first century...these annoying requirements of food and sleep should be voluntary by now."

"You're not superhuman, so please eat."

"Only to make you happy."

I loved food, sleep, and music, but he found them unnecessary inconveniences. I tried to imagine what life was like for him from his perspective. To not understand the basic things that made us human. Emotion. Enjoying a minuscule thing for the simple fact that it made you happy. In some ways, I felt sorry for him and the way he viewed the world.

I watched him eat slowly, small measured bites. When I was satisfied that he was going to eat what was on the plate, I went back to eating my own food. That didn't mean I didn't observe him. He seemed so out of place. A part of but so much alone, well, except for me. I'd discovered I had endless patience for his eccentricities.

Every time a customer walked in or out, his attention was drawn over my shoulder. He sized all of them up. He'd told me during one of our talks when we couldn't sleep that he assigned degrees of danger to everyone he met. I knew he was unarmed but I was confident that he'd protect me, he didn't need a weapon for that.

"It's safe here."

"It's my job to protect you and make sure you're safe. Let me do my job."

"Is that all I am...a job?" I asked cheekily.

The twitch of his eye warned me I was earning lashes. Every day we arrived home from work or going out, he'd tell me the tally. The punishment was just a speed bump in me getting my reward which ended up with him fucking me. I lived for the moments that he brought me pleasure and pain. Our lives together would never be easy and if it was, then what was the point?

"You're more than a job...you're mine."

"I'm happy with that."

"You better be. I plan on keeping you a very long time."

I grinned as I went back to eating and we lapsed into a comfortable silence. Listening to what was going on around me, the low drone of conversation while he remained on guard. Always prepared to keep me safe and happy.

AFTERMATH

Harrison

I hung from a hook that the chain of my handcuffs was draped over. My back was on fire, and every muscle in my body screamed in agony. I yelled at the last kiss of the whip against my back.

"Ten, thank you, sir." I counted as he requested and closed my eyes at the sting of sweat. I deserved my punishment. I hadn't trusted him to know what was best.

Just as my legs were about to go out, his arms were around me, and he was pressed flush to my back. I leaned my head back on his shoulder, and he soothed me— grounded me as my head went light.

"You made me so proud, boy."

With his arms around me, he helped me lift high enough to remove my tether to the hook. He walked me to the bathroom and sat me on the closed toilet seat. I kept my hands on him as he filled the tub, my head pressed to his ribs. I brushed a kiss to the deep valleyed scar where flesh was missing and another to the knife wound that had pierced his ribs. He'd gotten it as he had tried to save me when his old boss used me as leverage.

I'd spent days at his bedside as he'd turned repeatedly feverish. It was a reminder of how close I came to losing him. In the back of my brain, I still questioned sometimes why I stayed—why I didn't run as fast as possible.

He removed the cuffs, tugged me to my feet, and helped me into the tub. I hissed a bit as the warm water touched the stripes on my ass and lower back.

"Sh, I'll get you all cleaned up and then put your medicine on." He calmed me as he used a cup to wet my hair.

I sighed in pleasure as he worked shampoo through my hair and scored my scalp with his blunt nails.

"You still happy with me, sir?"

"Always, if not I'll find a beautiful place to spread your ashes."

I snorted as he said that with a straight face, but his gorgeous eyes brightened a bit. After a year, his joke delivery still needed some work. When I'd awakened in his basement clueless as to why and who had me, hell, even before, I'd never thought I'd be here.

The outside world would think something was wrong with my feelings for him and his for me. They didn't matter. I was truly happy for the first time in my life, and I wouldn't give it up for anything. I still spent nights and days alone as he took care of his new jobs. He required the killing to keep him grounded, and I wouldn't take that from him.

If anything, his routine was the hardest to adapt to—he was a creature of extreme habit. The only things he adjusted for were when he went on jobs. I'd learned a lot about him and the subtly of his surprise when he returned, and I was still there, broke me. As if I would leave him, I was addicted to and lost without him. Before him, my panic attacks were often, but since him, I rarely had them. They returned after Cristo had taken me. Although, it hadn't lasted long because he'd focused completely on me to give me my safety back.

That's what today's punishment was about. I hadn't come to him when the anxiety had taken over, and I'd attempted to suffer alone. He'd taken me in hand and given me the pain I needed to ground me, then cared for me as always. I hadn't understood what I needed until I'd met him. He'd shown me that I didn't need to be in control of everything—that he was there to always give me what I required.

He tilted my head back to strip the lather from my hair, and I watched him as he did. His cheek bore a new scar that heightened the harsh angles of his face. He wasn't beautiful or soft, and his expression never changed. Occasionally a smile would cause the tiniest tilt to one corner of his thin mouth.

I pouted my lips, and he gave me a quick kiss, then continued with his task of cleaning me from head to toe. His single-mindedness was extraordinary, and when we were together, it was always trained on me. I was his focal point, the place he didn't have to be on guard.

I stared at the cuff bracelet he'd given me months before, and I never removed it, sometimes he would grab my wrist at work. He's squeezed until the metal cut into my flesh. Just a bite of pain to remind me that he owned my pleasure, and more importantly, my pain.

"Do you love me, boy?"

"Yes, sir."

He roughly jerked my head back to stare into my eyes. "Say it, boy."

"I love you, sir."

I smiled up at him as the stiffness of his body eased, and his touch gentled. I wouldn't want to be anywhere else. Cowen was possessive, insane, unyielding, and homicidal, but I wouldn't have my crazy assassin any other way.

THE END

THANK YOU

Thank you for taking the time to read By Way of Pain. Cowen and Harrison were a labor of immense frustration, but I hope you enjoyed the tale I wove to get the psychopath his perfect boy.

MORE CRIMINAL DELIGHTS

Thank you for reading a CRIMINAL DELIGHTS novel.

For more deliciously dark tales, visit:
http://criminaldelights.com

Each novel can be read as a standalone and contains a dark M/M romance.

Books in the series:

K.A. Merikan
Wrong Way Home
Alex Jane
Devil Next Door
Katze Snow and Tiegan Clyne
Only the Devil Knows
L. A. Witt
Blood & Bitcoin
GB Gordon
Match Grade

Tal Bauer
Splintered
Michael Mandrake
Love Kills
Leona Windwalker
Beloved Possession
Sean Azinsalt
It's in My Blood
J.M. Dabney
By Way of Pain
Dora Esquivel
Hunters and Killers
M.D. Gregory
Sinner's Ransom
Michelle Frost
Cold Light
Abigail Kade
To Have and to Hold
Rorie Kage
His Final Curtain
Emma Jaye
Sweating Lies (Lies #1)
Emma Jaye
Splitting Lies (Lies #2)

ABOUT THE AUTHOR

J.M. Dabney is a multi-genre author who writes mainly LGBT romance and fiction. They live with a constant diverse cast of characters in their head. No matter their size, shape, race, etc. J.M. lives for one purpose alone, and that's to make sure they do them justice and give them the happily ever after they deserve. J.M. is dysfunction at its finest and they makes sure their characters are a beautiful kaleidoscope of crazy. There is nothing more they want from telling their stories than to show that no matter the package the characters come in or the damage their pasts have done, that love is love. That normal is never normal and sometimes the so-called broken can still be amazing.

Reader Group –
https://www.facebook.com/groups/585182991553194/

Mailing List – http://eepurl.com/dzWnIn

facebook.com/J.M.DabneyAuthor

twitter.com/jmdabney_author

instagram.com/authorjmdabney

amazon.com/B006QZIFLE

The Hunt

J.M. Dabney & Davidson King

Disgraced detective turned private investigator, Ray Clancy, left the force with a case unsolved. Finding the killer was no longer his problem, but it still haunted him. How long would he survive the frustration of not knowing before he gave into the compulsion of his nature to solve the crime?

Server, Andrew Shay, existed where he didn't feel he belonged, living behind the guise of a costume. Yet it paid the bills, and he refused to complain about the little things in life. One night he returned home from work to find his roommate dead and the killer still there. Afraid and alone, his life spiraled and he didn't know what to do. Could a detective at his core and a scared young man join forces to bring down the killer in their midst?

Universal Link - books2read.com/JM-Dabney-Davidson-King1